SUMMER ROMANCE

Samantha Beauchamp's trip to Corfu is a chance to start a new life – romance is the last thing on her mind. But when she meets local entrepreneur Rhexenor Gaia she finds herself alternately fascinated and enraged by his mercurial nature and arrogance. However, Rhex is out of bounds, soon to marry the beautiful Cassiami, and Samantha decides that any interest he shows her is merely due to his previous friendship with her father.

Samantha has the attentions of gentle and uncomplicated historian Ben Mathers to keep her occupied, but who will ultimately restore her faith in men?

SUMMER ROMANCE

SUMMER ROMANCE

by

Elizabeth Daish

Magna Large Print Books
Long Preston, North Yorkshire,
BD23 4ND, England.

British Library Cataloguing in Publication Data.

Daish, Elizabeth
    Summer romance.

    A catalogue record of this book is
    available from the British Library

    ISBN   0-7505-1568-6

First published in Great Britain by
Hamlyn Publishing Group Ltd., 1983

Published in Large Print 2001 by arrangement with
Severn House Publishers Ltd.

Magna Large Print is an imprint of Library Magna Books Ltd.

Printed and bound in Great Britain by
T.J. (International) Ltd., Cornwall, PL28 8RW

1

'I'm very sorry, Madam.' Samantha stared at the woman in utter disbelief. 'I'm very sorry,' Eva said in a slightly less belligerent tone. 'The rooms, they are taken and I have no others except those in our so very good annexe. Along the beach ... a little, little way along the beach.'

'Do you mean that house with broken shutters and peeling paint at least half a mile away on a piece of scrubland? The one we passed on the way from the airport? You have to be joking!' Samantha thrust a hot hand through her thick dark hair and shifted on the hard chair, longing for a cool shower, a cool drink and a room; the room she had booked, with a balcony overlooking the sea. She particularly wanted to be in this small clean taverna in the north of Corfu.

Eva moved her huge bulk, sending waves of scent from the billowing cotton dress. She looked cool and business-like and reminded Samantha of a cuddly bear who sensed she was less than popular. 'I'm very sorry.' She waved a hand, and as if on cue, a goodlooking waiter slid into the café area of the taverna with a tray of drinks. Eva looked at the array of fizzy soft drinks. 'You have this on the house,' she said, beaming hopefully. She took the metal cap from a bottle and put a green drinking straw into the pink fluid.

'I don't want it,' gritted Samantha. 'I want a room, a shower and some food. In that order. You know you had my booking and my cheque, and you said that I could have the same room that my father had when he was here two years ago, so there is no doubt in my mind that you understood the situation perfectly. I don't know what my father will say. He will be disappointed, to say the least.'

'Ah, yes, the Kyrie Beauchamp.' The smile

disappeared, as if she had just recalled the fact that the famous John Beauchamp, champion racing driver, had stayed in the tiny village and had telephoned her all the way from England to ask her to make his daughter comfortable during her holiday in Corfu.

'You double-booked,' accused Samantha.

'No, that is not true. I...' Eva blushed. 'The taverna is owned by someone who is here sometimes, but never during this month. He uses that room when he comes...'

'And he changed his mind and wants it. Tell me,' said Samantha, sarcastically, 'does he know that you make a bit on the side hiring out his room when he isn't here?'

'He knows, but he expects to have his room whenever he needs it.'

'And the poor fools who come here are thrown out to the waste land, to suit the whims of one selfish man who hasn't the decency to send a cable giving you due notice of his coming. He must know in advance to be able to book an air passage!'

'An air passage, madam? It is not necessary. Kyrie Gaia lives on Corfu and comes here to sail and to fish.' She looked at the pale-faced girl with the huge sad eyes that seemed about to fill with tears of utter weariness. 'You are like your father, so good to look on, so sad... I will give you my rooms.' Eva chuckled. 'Of course! I can give you a room in my villa! There is one young woman only there and the other booking was cancelled. It is pretty and better than this.' The sweep of her plump hand dismissed the spotless taverna as worthless and she stood up and moved briskly to the open doorway. 'Iannis, bring the bags of the Kyria.' Samantha followed, slowly, uncertain whether to accept the offer or to insist on her rights, but she was too hot and tired to do anything but follow the woman, who walked along the seafront for fifty yards and paused by an outside stairway that led up to the first floor of an old villa overlooking the sea. Eva heaved herself up the creaking stairs and Samantha went up after her, to a wooden landing with a blue painted door, which the woman unlocked.

Inside was a tiny hallway, from which rooms radiated. Eva unlocked a door and went into a bedroom, flinging wide the wooden shutters over the windows and flooding the room with bright white sunlight.

'It's lovely,' said Samantha. She gazed out at the vivid blue sea that lapped at a wall under the window. The bed was covered with a clean coverlet of washed-out pastels, and the subdued colours were echoed in the rugs on the polished floorboards. A slight breeze stirred the fine muslin curtains at the wide windows. A small shower room and toilet made a self-contained unit.

Eva stood with her hands on her ample hips. 'It is good. Your father will be pleased?' She sounded anxious, and Samantha smiled for the first time since her arrival. 'Ah, now you are *very* like the Kyrie Beauchamp. He has a pretty smile, too. You come for meals

11

at the taverna, and because you are not pleased at first, you have wine with me tonight.' She gave Samantha two keys: one for the outer door and one for her bedroom. Iannis brought up the baggage and ran down the stairs again to get back to his job at the bar. Eva opened a door to show Samantha a small sitting room. 'You share this with the other lady, if you wish.' Eva smiled and concentrated on negotiating the outer stairway safely. 'Eat at nine with me, but come for something small – and drinks, anything – when you are unpacked.' Her voice faded as she reached the quayside and ambled back to the taverna.

Samantha tested the shower and found that it worked perfectly, with good hot water and adequate controls. She stripped off, after locking the bedroom door, and the soft warm water and scented soap soothed her hot tired body. On an impulse, she let the water flow through her hair, luxuriating in the sensation of fluid warmth running down her face and neck and caressing her smooth body, and totally disregarding the fact that her hair would be wet for ages after this treatment as she had no drier with her, and the dense mass of shining dark hair would be damp even when she went to dinner at nine.

Cool and more relaxed than she had been for hours, days – or was it weeks? – she tipped the contents of one of her cases on the bed and surveyed her clothes. She picked up a dark green dress and frowned. It had looked ordinary and passable at home, but in the bright sunlight of her room, it was dowdy and just not right. 'Who cares? There's nobody here to see me,' she said defiantly, and struggled into it. After almost living in jeans and sweaters at home, she had forgotten that the dress was so short and simple. I haven't worn it for years, she thought. I look like a Girl Guide on a camping trip. With wet flat hair and the dull dress, she could indeed have passed for a teenager with long legs and slight hips, although the gentle curves of her bosom gave a promise of womanhood. Almost angrily, she added flat sandals to complete the illusion. What did it matter how she looked? Who cared if she looked a mess? She leaned out of the window to let the sun dry her hair, and she could see the sandy beach in front of the few shops, the odd villa or two, a café and the taverna, stretching away to the misty headland where sea and sky were a hazy blue. She took a deep breath and relaxed. Out over the windless sea two small fishing boats floated, their sails limp. She heard an outboard engine start and one of the sails came down. She looked again and saw another craft. She shaded her eyes and peered out to sea. The twin hulls of a catamaran were coming under power, straight for the shore by the taverna.

Samantha stared and, as the boat came closer, she could see a figure standing by the wheel. The late afternoon sun slanted down across the water, bringing silver lights among the gold and blue. The same shafts brought a glowing halo to the hair of the man who stood still and tall, with shining tanned shoulders, narrow waist and firm strong thighs. His hair was curled and thick, gleaming with a fine spray of salt water, which darkened the auburn glow but made his face seem craggy and almost cruel as he gripped the wheel and then bent to cut the engine. The boat glided into shallow water and the ring of the mooring buoy was expertly hooked and made fast.

A door slammed but Samantha took no notice. That face – she had seen that face somewhere. She craned her neck and nearly fell out of the window in her efforts to see him again, but the rubber dinghy that he flung from the boat was on the other side and his progress to the shore was hidden by the awning of the taverna beach bar. 'Prospero,' she said, and smiled.

She was still smiling as she answered the knock on the door. 'Hello, are you Eva's other lady?' she asked.

'I'm Carla Andrews,' said the fair-haired

girl who stood smiling in the doorway. She laughed. 'Gee, how relieved I am to see you! I wondered who I was getting as a neighbour.' She eyed Samantha with frank curiosity and some amusement. 'When you've finished dripping, how about a drink? I'll give you ten minutes if you want to change.'

'I am changed,' said Samantha. 'That is, I came away in a hurry and don't seem to have brought anything suitable for this place.' She stopped before she apologised for her appearance but felt more self-conscious than she had thought possible. 'I'm Samantha Beauchamp, from England. I'll just give my hair another rub and then it can dry in the sun.'

'And as you can tell from my accent, I'm from Texas, in God's own country!' She chuckled. 'You look about twelve in that rig. Do you always dress like that?'

It was impossible to take offence and Samantha laughed. 'It's a long story. I may or may not tell it to you, but I'm glad to meet you. Do you mind if we call in at the shops on the way? I must buy some light clothes.'

'You on the run or something? No clothes and having to buy fresh?'

In a way, I suppose I am on the run, she thought. 'I just came away in a hurry and seem to have brought some things that are too formal for this place and some rather thick jeans and tops. I don't think I own more than two summer dresses and a skirt, so let's see the local haute couture.'

They riffled through the line of cotton garments hanging from the shopfront by the café and, in spite of her earlier indifference to what she wore, Samantha found that the enthusiasm of the American girl was infectious. She chose a wide skirt of soft pink cotton and bought a pale green tee-shirt and a pretty white lace blouse, then paused by a heavy cotton and lace dress in pale coffee and cream. It had a low-cut neckline and close-fitting bodice and the shopkeeper

17

encouraged her to try it on at the villa at her leisure and to change it if it didn't fit.

'I'll take it,' she said, recklessly. After all, this holiday was the end of one era; wasn't it only fair to try to start afresh?

She carried the clothes with her to the taverna. 'I'm dying for a long cool drink. I'll try these on later before dinner, but I shall die of thirst if I don't have something cool in just two minutes,' she said.

Carla began to tell her about the tiny village, from the superiority that two days' stay in the place had given her. 'Just the taverna for meals and drinks and lovely shade when it's very hot,' she said. Samantha glanced at the too-fair skin that looked vulnerable to over-exposure in the sun and was glad that she had no problem with tanning. Her skin, she knew, would turn a deep golden brown within days of the first session in the sun, with no hint of burning. 'I can do with some coffee,' said Carla.

'In this heat? I can't wait to get some sun and I intend cooling off with cold drinks every hour, on the hour,' said Samantha.

'You tan easily? Lucky you. But you do look a bit pale now. Have you been ill?' Carla asked shrewdly.

'Not exactly... Just busy.' Samantha studied the menu and chose a glass of fresh orange juice with lots of ice. Iannis brought it quickly, obviously knowing that Eva would be cross if the younger Kyria was annoyed again. His practised eyes surveyed her from head to foot and dismissed her as unlikely to be seeking a holiday romance with a handsome Greek waiter. He made corny jokes with Carla, who treated him with mild tolerance and faint amusement, and then he gave up and directed his charm towards two middle-aged women, who greeted him as a long-lost friend.

Samantha sipped the cool drink and looked out to sea. 'Did you see the cat?' said Carla.

'The cat? No, does it belong to Eva?'

'Not as in animal – that one.' Carla pointed to the catamaran which swayed gently at the mooring. 'Beautiful, isn't she?' She sighed. 'I'd love to go out on her, but Eva says it's impossible. Belongs to the boss-who-can-do-no-wrong.' She swung her legs over the side of her chair so that they dangled above the sand beneath the platform on which the tables were set. 'Can't make up my mind to swim. If I do, I'll have to wash my hair.' She looked at Samantha's wet hair. 'At least your hair is thick. Mine looks like rat's tails when it's wet and I just have to put it in rollers.'

'Why not have it cut really short? It would suit you.' It was becoming easier and easier to talk naturally to the fair-haired girl who had been unknown to her only an hour or two ago. England and all that remained there of everything she loved and hated was far away and receding swiftly. A rush and flurry of sand made Samantha look up. A red setter dog with gleaming coat and lolling tongue scattered sand under the awning and stood waiting as if expecting to be chased. 'He's beautiful,' said Samantha.

'Which one, the dog or his master?' Carla gave a low whistle, and the dog looked at her. He hesitated and she whistled again. Head down, he came to her and let her reach down to smooth his ears.

'Ariel!' The voice was deep and very masculine. The dog jumped up to be near his new friends and nuzzled Samantha's toes, rubbing his wet fur along the line of her bare leg. *'Ariel!'* The voice was imperious and tinged with annoyance. The dog took no notice but licked Carla's hand. A shadow fell across the table as a powerful hand stretched down to the dog and took him by the collar. The setter shook himself, sending a circle of spray over the two girls, and the man with the haloed hair frowned. 'My apologies,' he said to Carla. 'He is young and not yet trained.' He ignored the young girl who sat with the American woman, a visiting child, a colourless girl with dull long hair and pale cheeks in a ridiculous garment that passed for a dress.

'Come, Ariel. Bad dog. We run.' He

pushed the dog towards the beach and followed, running and chasing like a god along the golden sand. The glow of sunset sent faint echoes of peach and rose to his damp skin and bright hair. The muscles of his shoulders and back were visible under the brown skin, and against the light he looked naked, clad as he was in the smallest of trunks. Samantha smoothed the damp patch on her arm where the salt-wet hand of the man had touched as he bent towards the dog. It seemed to glow with his brightness, and there was no sensation of cold or wet, just a tingling of contact, of a one-way electric impulse that stung and yet did not repel.

'Ariel – of course.' Samantha laughed and Carla looked at her in amazement. 'I saw him from the window and thought he was Prospero, and Prospero has his Ariel.'

'Are you crazy? Who is Prospero? Right now the only man we have seen except for Iannis is Mr Gaia, Eva's boss.'

'He – he is Mr Gaia? The man who took

my room? I might have known.' Samantha recalled the way his eyes had slid over her, not registering the fact that she existed, certainly not as a woman. Just the kind of thing he would do. 'Anyone can see that he's an arrogant beast used to getting everything his own way.'

'But beautiful,' said Carla.

'I didn't notice,' said Samantha. 'But I liked the dog.'

'What is this Prospero thing?'

'Don't they teach you Shakespeare in America?' Samantha laughed, trying to forget the twist of the man's mouth in half-admitted humour, the clearness of eyes that would never see her as a woman and the touch that had shocked her with its intense animal attraction. 'Prospero was ship-wrecked on an island – believed to be Corfu – and he had a sprite called Ariel who did his bidding. There was magic and adventure and a monster called Caliban... Perhaps I should have called Mr Gaia Caliban.' She put her head on one side. 'No, arrogant he may be, but he has to be Prospero. You should read *The Tempest* some time.'

'I think I did, years ago, but I'll take your word for it. The name suits him. I wonder what he'll say when he hears you think of him as Prospero?'

'You wouldn't tell him?' Carla chuckled. 'Of course, you're teasing. We shan't see him in the taverna. Eva said he had all his meals sent up to his room.'

'Oh, does he? I was looking forward to seeing the vultures trying to get at him. Might have been quite entertaining.' She nodded towards the two women who sat alone in the corner, watching everyone and everything that happened, intent on squeezing the last drop of enjoyment from their holiday even if some of their pleasure had to be at second hand. 'They're nice even if they're a bit homely,' said Carla, 'and Iannis gives them the odd languorous look, which is good for a cheap thrill.'

'He's very good-looking,' said Samantha, 'but I think he knows just who will be interested in him and those who have no such thoughts in their heads.'

'And you have no such thoughts? With all this sun and blue seas and, later, the music? What gives, Sam? I would hardly call you the nunlike type. A woman on her own who isn't looking for a little … diversion? Come on, tell me what turns you on.'

Samantha drained her glass and her eyes darkened with remembered pain. 'I came to get away, not to add to my troubles,' she said in a low voice.

'I'm sorry. Don't look like that, Sam. Can I call you that? Samantha is such a prudy little mouthful, and Sam suits you better.'

'Call me what you like. Sam is fine.' She curled her lip wryly. 'I might as well get used to being called Sam again, and what better place than this?'

'Come on, you sound hungry. When a pretty girl weeps into her orange juice, it's time to feed her. Now, me … take me; I refuse to be depressed at anything any more. Come on, we'll get you into one of those outfits and stuff our faces.'

Carla gathered up the bundles of clothes and walked away, leaving Sam to follow her. For a moment, she stared at the headland, where the shell pink of sunset was practising on the edges of a cloud. The headland was barren and ochre yellow, with tufts of hard scrub looking like the untrimmed beard of a giant lying at sleep, but there was no human movement on the shore. Mr Gaia and his dog had gone. She wondered if he would be staying for more than a day or so, and hurried after Carla, determined to dismiss him from her mind. If he goes, I can have my room, she thought, and made an effort to convince herself that her only interest in him lay in the fact that she wanted her room with a balcony.

'Just look at that sky,' said Samantha when Carla put the packages on the bed. 'He can keep the room. Eva was right, and I wouldn't change now if she offered me the room I booked.' She shook out the clothes and placed them out on the bed. 'I'll try them on and be ready in half an hour, if that's all right with you, Carla.'

'I need a shower – see you later.' And Samantha heard the shower flowing and a muffled rendering of the latest pop song coming from the other girl's room.

Both tops went with the skirt, and they would be fine with jeans too. At least I have a couple of new bikinis and some shorts for the beach, Samantha thought, and I can buy some light cotton trousers if we go walking through the spiky grass and bushes. Her pulse quickened, and she realised that she was enjoying being in the charming room, being in Corfu and having the companionship of a new friend who took life lightly and would make no great demands on her. She held the coffee and cream dress up against her body. It was very pretty. She slipped it over her head and smoothed it down over her hips. It fitted closely over her bosom, dipping to show her cleavage sufficiently to hint at the gentle curves under the bodice, then clung to her tiny waist and flowed freely from her hips. The heavy cotton moulded to her body and moved with her, first touching then flowing away from the long slim line of her thighs.

Samantha brushed her hair and let it flow over her shoulders as it was still slightly damp, but the dry surface layer glowed with health and blue-black lights. She touched her eyelids with faint tinges of blue which made the grey blue turn to a deeper colour, and applied a rich rosy lipstick. The shoes she had worn from England looked much too solid, and she chose a pair of pretty sandals that she had bought a long time ago and never worn. Am I changing already? she wondered. Can this place possess a magic that is working even at this early stage of my holiday? The girl with thick dark hair flowing over her shoulders was so different from the fraught young woman who had left England with her mouth tight and her hair caught back in an ugly elastic band so rigidly controlled that she looked like a very cross schoolmistress.

She rubbed cream into her hands and looked out at the sunset while the pop song and the shower reached the final crescendo.

This time yesterday I was at home, she thought. It had been raining and the driveway from the garage was flooded again. Samantha touched the warmth of her bare arm and could hardly believe that she had been huddled in a thick raincoat, jeans and rubber boots while she took a yard broom and swept away the accumulation of water from the forecourt. 'Sam!' Her father had called, and she rested the broom against one of the petrol pumps to go into the house. 'Have you seen my pocket calculator?' he asked.

'It's in the office where you always put it,' she said, patiently. 'Do you really think you can manage if I go away? What will you do if you haven't got me to run after you?' Her tone was light but she didn't smile.

'I shall manage very well. Now, just you leave that job. Don can finish it. You get

29

packed and make sure you have everything you need. It's time you had a break, Samantha, and there's nothing here that can't be done by others now.' He limped slightly as he walked across the hall to the office, and Samantha marvelled at the mobility of the man who had been picked from the wreckage of his high-powered racing car three years ago almost in pieces himself. She saw the lines etched by pain and frustration and her glance softened. Poor Dad, he had suffered so much, both in body and mind, and the brilliant career that had been his right had crumbled overnight, leaving him to the surgeons, the physiotherapists and Samantha, his daughter, who gave up her job with a London export and import business to nurse him – and will him – back to active life.

John Beauchamp poured himself a generous drink. He waved the decanter in the air but she shook her head. That was another thing she had fought: the reliance of a disappointed man on escape through drinking, wild company and even drugs. She smiled. 'It isn't me who has to get organised. Have you made out that list of orders yet?'

'That's why I wanted the calculator. I've got everything under control, Samantha. Thanks to you,' he added, awkwardly. He had studiously refused to meet her gaze since she came into the house. 'Sit down. I have to say it once before you leave. I'm sorry.' She stiffened. 'I know...' He held up a hand as if to ward off her fury. 'I promised never to refer to it again and to turn over a few new leaves, but now you're going, I suddenly realised just how much you have had to put up with here.'

'There's no need to rake up what is best forgotten,' she said. 'If you want to make amends, forget it and let me forget it too.'

'But I thought you liked him, Samantha. He came here often enough and I believed him when he said he wanted to marry you. He *did* ask you, didn't he?'

'He came often enough, as you said,' she

agreed, bitterly. 'He came to your drunken parties and, like some of your other dear friends, he wanted other entertainment...'

'You should have told me. You never said that they tried anything. My God, Samantha, they–'

'Don't worry, Dad. Even though it's a little late now.' Her dark eyes flashed contempt. 'Twice I had to fight off some drunken lout who tried to kiss me, and then Max...' Her eyes filled with tears, re-membering the night when her father had collapsed on his bed after an evening drinking with the friends from the racing pits and she had found herself alone with the man whom she had trusted, had begun to think she could marry. Even now, she could almost smell the stale spirit on his hot breath as he came towards her; she could recall the iron grip as he held her close and fumbled for her skirt zip, the rampant lust in his eyes filling her with such fear and disgust that she took up a pair of scissors from a table and fought him off, knowing that he intended rape. She had fled and locked herself in, leaving him to explain the scratches and cuts from her weapon.

'You know he came the next day, and actually proposed?' her voice was brittle with disgust. 'He even hinted that he preferred me now he knew I had a bit of spirit.'

Her father shrugged, helplessly. 'It should never have happened and I can't begin to say how sorry I am.' His dark eyes, a darker blue but so like her own, were pleading. 'I shall miss you, Samantha. Don't forget to come back.'

'I'll be back and then we'll talk again. I still want to leave this place and have a flat of my own. I'll take the holiday as you've gone to the trouble to ring your friend Eva, but it alters nothing. I shall come back and start again with a job in London and a place of my own.' She smiled, with more warmth in her eyes. 'You're young. You should get married again. It's five years since mother died, and women still find you very attractive.'

'I know I'm a bit more straight in my affairs and mind, but that...' He shook his head. 'Come back here, Samantha, and you can run things exactly as you want them. You can have this house divided, if that would make it easier, and never meet any of the lads again.' She shook her head. 'You *will* come back?'

'I shall come back to clear up here and find what I need, and then we'll see. By that time, you might have a wife in mind. Don't tell me you wouldn't like to be married? I'll pack now and say goodnight. It's a dawn start for me, so I'll drive to the airport and Don can collect the car later.'

'Samantha.' She turned at the door. 'Take this.' He handed her an envelope. 'It might come in useful. You never buy clothes. Is it because you are afraid to look attractive here?' She shook her head, but he saw the flush of shame. 'I must have been mad. I've been a mad, selfish, uncomprehending fool.' She remained with her hands at her side. 'Take it. For God's sake take it, Samantha.

At least let me try to make it up to you. Buy some pretty things... Make new friends... Leave me if you must, but don't leave me with this terrible burden of guilt.'

She took the fat envelope and stuffed it into her pocket. 'Goodbye,' she said. 'Money doesn't buy everything, but I bear you no malice, even though I could never be the son you wanted.'

'Sam...'

'Don't call me that. *He* used that name when he was being his most charming. I'm not your son Sam. I'm a woman called Samantha.' She swept from the room, eyes brimming with the tears she refused to shed. I've shed enough tears, she thought. Tears because I could never follow him as a racing driver, never have his full attention or his love, and more tears because he refused to understand the needs of a daughter.

In her room, she flung the damp clothes away and packed, throwing in anything that came to hand. In the packet of money, she found another envelope with a piece of card on which was stuck a coin. 'This Greek coin is from Corfu. It was found in the folds of upholstery in the old Bugatti a few years ago. Take it for good luck, Samantha, my dear daughter.' And at last the tears flowed, washing away her hate but leaving her numb and empty.

'Ready?' Carla's voice sang through the door.

'Ready,' said Samantha.

'What's that? It looks old,' said Carla.

'I found it in my case. It's Greek. From Corfu, or so I'm told.' Samantha held up the coin so that it glinted dully in the light. 'My father found it a long time ago.'

'Here? Did he come here?' Carla turned it over.

'No. He hadn't been here for years until a couple of years ago when he came to rest with some friends. He found it in an old car that he wanted to restore, a rather lovely old Bugatti.'

'Do you see? It has a tortoise on this side.

It's real cute. I wonder if I can get some to send home?'

'I think the turtle was an emblem in use here in ancient times. They have turtles and terrapins here, I think, inland in the streams.' Samantha looked puzzled, wondering where she had heard those words and who had said them to her when she was still at school.

'Well, I could eat a whole big turtle, or a tortoise, and crunch up the shell,' said Carla. They locked the doors carefully and went down the sighing stairs. 'You look a different girl. Quite the transformation scene. I wish my hair was dark and glowing and mysterious.'

'Nothing mysterious about me,' said Samantha. 'I'll tell you all, but not tonight. I want to get to know this place, and I think I'm going to enjoy it.'

Eva beckoned and sat them by the window overlooking the sea. 'I save for you because you are not cross with me.' She handed them the menu. 'We eat, but I get up sometimes. You choose and for tonight you are my guests.' She looked at Samantha's dress with amused approval. 'Our young women wear and look good, but you look better.' She glanced at the slim waist. 'It was made for you. You are like Princess Nausicaa.' Her huge body shook with laughter at some secret joke and she stood up quickly to go to the kitchens, where raised voices could be heard.

Iannis and Eva were almost shouting at another of the waiters. The rapid Greek was beyond even Carla's knowledge of the language and it stopped as suddenly as it began, giving way to light laughter. Carla shrugged. 'It happens all the time. They bawl at each other and then laugh. They are the most good-tempered people.'

'Everything all right?' asked Carla, when Eva came back.

'Of course,' said Eva in surprise, and gave the order for food to Iannis who stood smiling at Samantha as if he had just seen a vision.

'Is Mr Gaia dining here?' said Carla.

'No,' said Eva. 'He is on the boat with Stavros. They mend it.' She shrugged. 'He fishes with Stavros and bring lobster for Maik. He sails and runs with the dog and sleeps here.' She giggled. 'He is a pretty man, yes?'

'I wouldn't know,' said Samantha.

'Ah, you are still cross about the room. He should be sorry.'

'It doesn't matter really. I love the room in the villa and I wouldn't want to change back.'

Samantha gave her full attention to the delicious grilled fish and Greek salad and the warm fresh bread. The relief she had anticipated at the thought of his absence didn't surface. The people at the other tables lacked any aura, lacked the radiance that seemed to follow the man with the beautiful red setter. 'Where do we go after this?' said Samantha, in a determined effort to dismiss the arrogant but compelling man from her thoughts. 'Any night life?'

'We go to Maik's café,' said Carla firmly.

'You don't have to entertain me all the time,' said Samantha. 'You must have friends you want to meet.

'Not a soul. Isn't it great? I came away on my own to be alone, but if you can stand me for more than two hours at a time, I'll be delighted.'

The last spoonful of ice-cream disappeared and Eva left the table to make sure that all was well in the back regions. 'If we want to go to Maik's, let's go before I fall asleep. I shall go to bed soon, but you won't disturb me if you come back late.' Samantha yawned.

'You have to have at least one ouzo or a metaxa, the Greek brandy, with some coffee,' Carla insisted. So they walked past the shuttered houses and the shop where the last of the dresses was being taken in for the night.

The café was half full as the pretty wife of the owner came to take their orders. Softly,

Greek music wafted through the room and the buzz of conversation almost hid it. The people at the tables were mostly local Corfiots and the atmosphere was warm and friendly. The music grew louder as the café filled. The young men lit fresh cigarettes to droop from their lips and they formed a line, shoulder to shoulder. They danced the deceptively simple steps of the sirtaki with natural grace and complete control. It was young and natural and as old as the hills. Samantha drank her ouzo and wondered why she had never come to Corfu before. With slightly parted lips she turned to make a remark to Carla. The light shone on her hair as she pushed stray strands back from her face, giving it the blue-black lustre of a raven's wing. She bent forward and the gentle lines of her figure rose and fell, slightly breathlessly, and the man who stood in the doorway watching the dance looked at her with narrowed eyes as if trying to remember where he had seen her.

'I must go, or I'll never climb those stairs,'

said Samantha.

'I'm tired, too. Let's get up early and swim before the day starts.' Carla picked up her handbag and walked towards the door.

The man from the catamaran lounged against the doorpost, dressed in a silk shirt of dark blue and tightly fitting trousers of natural linen. His masculinity was no less now that he was fully clothed, and his eyes held appraisal, insolence and amusement. Samantha felt his eyes like laser beams destroying her clothes, her pride and her resistance. She passed within inches of his shoulder and hoped quite desperately that she wasn't blushing, as her heart began to beat rapidly. She didn't know whether she wanted to turn and slap the insolence from his face, or to touch the mobile mouth with a gentle finger.

2

'What a gruesome sight!' said Carla. Samantha sat on a rock and picked a shred of seaweed from between her toes. 'Not your feet – that hotel. I didn't walk all this way or paddle round the headland just to see a mass of concrete.'

'It's what is described as a luxury hotel, and there are very many people who might prefer it to our tiny taverna.' Samantha gazed at the bright umbrellas on the terrace by the hotel pool. 'Not that I like huge hotels,' she added.

'I hate them,' said Carla. 'I was brought up in them. My family moved about a lot in the States and dragged me with them. After a while, it's difficult to know which hotel is which and even to know which town we hit.' She looked sad for the first time since

Samantha met her twenty-four hours earlier.

'So you made sure of a small place for your holiday?'

'Like you, I had to get away to think out the next phase in my life.' She stretched and smiled. 'Let's not go there for drinks. I'd rather walk back along the shore and see what Iannis can concoct for us. I just love my little room and all those crazy stairs. I wonder where all the boats have gone? Did you hear them late last night? A man was shouting soon after we got to bed.'

'I didn't hear a thing. I sank into bed and that was all I knew until you banged on the door this morning.'

'You didn't hear the dog barking?'

'The dog? There must be several dogs here and I suppose they all have to bark at some time,' said Samantha, trying not to think of one dog with a bright red coat and a man pursuing him along a sandy shore wearing so little that she couldn't look at him without blushing.

'Oh, you know this one. I looked out and saw Mr Gaia was rowing out to the cat, with the dog in the stern. One of the fishing boats had lights on the masthead to lure the fish, so I suppose they were going out for a night's fishing.' Carla climbed down to the beach and walked back along the shore line. 'Let's go inland a bit to explore on the way back. It will give our sandals time to dry out. I wish we could walk barefooted but Eva warned me of spiky-spined fish that lie under the surface of the sand and cause a nasty wound if the spines break off under the skin.'

'Do you think it's a coincidence that the local shop just happens to stock rubber sandals? Does Eva get a rake-off on sales?' Samantha laughed and reached up to thrust back her long hair. The ribbon with which she had tied it in a Mozart bow at the back of her head was slipping, so she removed it and crumpled it into a ball, thrusting it into the pocket of her red shorts. It was good to walk freely in the hot sun in brief shorts and a white strapless top with the warm air a caress on her bare shoulders.

'It's not fair,' said Carla, who had a red tip to her nose and pink patches on her arms already. 'I could go off you! Yesterday, you looked pale and vaguely unwell, and today you not only glow with health, but your hair and skin look wonderful and from somewhere you have found a beautiful body!'

'It's all done by mirrors,' said Samantha. 'I think it's because I'm really relaxed, the sun is shining and in my last life I was a sun worshipper.'

'I think I lived in the Arctic as a polar bear or a penguin, or some other creature allergic to heat.' Carla grinned. 'Was it only the sun you worshipped? How about a handsome Greek god or two? I've seen one or two faces here straight from ancient vases – our Mr Gaia for one – and in his own way, Iannis has a classic look about him even though he'll never be anything but a small time hustler in a tiny village.'

'No, Mr Gaia isn't my type. He's too sure

of himself and much too theatrical. It's a pose, running about with a dog that is so beautiful he's bound to get attention.'

'My my! What *has* the poor man done? Could it be that sultry look he gave you last night that upset your nice puritanical soul?'

'Last night? You must have drunk too much ouzo.' Samantha climbed the bank onto the white dusty path above the beach that led back through olive groves and lemon orchards.

The cool shade was dark and Carla sighed with relief. 'Let's walk back this way and go over the bridge we can see from the villa windows.' The sleepy buzz of many flying insects made the heat outside the trees seem even more soporific and they idled, picking leaves from the bushes to discover which were aromatic herbs that the locals used for cooking. Small poppies hung silken heads over wild thyme, and tall fronds of fennel smelled faintly of aniseed. A woman dressed from head to foot in black passed with a small donkey laden with vegetables.

'Kalimera,' said Samantha, shyly.

'Kalimera,' said the woman, and smiled.

'They like to be greeted,' said Carla. 'I tried to brush up my Greek before I came but I find I can't understand Eva when she gets going with Iannis.'

'My limit is hello, goodbye, good evening and how much?' said Samantha, 'but it seems to be enough. I've heard that most Greeks know a little English, so that shopping will be OK.'

They came to the tiny hump-backed bridge that lay on the land side of the path. The stream that flowed under it stopped short in a pool about fifty yards inland with no outlet to the sea. 'Must be a fresh water pool. I wonder if it connects with the sea during the winter rains,' said Carla. 'Oh, what's that? Not a water rat ... I hate rats.'

'No, it's broader and heavier. It's a turtle,' said Samantha, in wonder. 'Does it live in fresh water, or was it left from the last flood and got stranded from the sea?'

'We'll never know, but look, there's

another ... and another and the grandfather over there. The stream is teeming with them,'

Samantha gazed down through the weed fringing the stream. 'The turtles of Corfu,' she said, softly. 'Still here after all these centuries.' She felt a warmth of familiarity towards the ungainly creatures that swam so gracefully, as if flying under water, surfacing to stare at the shadows cast by the two women. A child rushed from the path leading to the village and climbed the bridge. She threw pieces of stale bread into the water and the turtles surfaced to eat it. There were at least a dozen of the shiny shellbacks vying for the bigger pieces of bread.

'I wish I'd saved my bread this morning,' said Samantha. 'I must bring some tomorrow.' The markings on the grey and brown backs were like the ones on the turtle of the coin. *Take it to bring you luck*, her father had written. But what luck could they bring her, apart from this breathing space in a wonderful place?

They walked back to the village and sank into chairs under the taverna awning. Samantha gazed out at the horizon and wondered what fishermen did during the day. She glanced up at the balcony of the room that Mr Gaia occupied, but the shutters were closed. He might be asleep up there after a night out on the sea, but if so, where was the catamaran? 'Iannis, something long and very cold, like a beer,' she said.

The sea lay dark blue and as dense as a pool of mercury. Sand, brought in from the beach on the bare feet of swimmers and left drying in patches on the tiled floor, softened into heaps of gold dust, and the broad leaves of Eva's pot plants glistened as she poured precious water over them, and even at lunch time, the faint sound of music filtered from shuttered windows. They ordered salad and moussaka, suddenly hungry, and Iannis brought fresh Greek bread. There was little for him to do as most of the guests had gone into Corfu town in the bus. He hovered, ready to talk and wanting to make an impression on the girls. 'You have everything you want?' he asked.

'Yes, thank you. Everything is fine,' said Carla.

'You will want to go into Corfu town?' The girls exchanged glances. 'You need a car,' he said, firmly. 'It is beautiful in Corfu. Many shops, many cars, much to see.'

Samantha wrinkled her nose. 'Free exhaust fumes? I can wait for that.'

'But it's not a bad idea. Do you drive, Sam?' Samantha smiled, wondering what Carla would say if she knew that she was almost as good a driver as her famous father. She nodded. 'We could hire one for a day or so and see something of the mountains. It would be cooler up there in the afternoons.'

'If you want a car, ask Stavros. He has a garage and cars. Stavros takes visitors if you do not drive. Stavros hires cars, hires boats.

You have something to mend, Stavros he fix it.'

'This Stavros is a very busy man,' said Samantha dryly.

'You want to go to the mountains,' said Iannis, 'so you need a car. No bus to the mountains. Not for you,' he added. He saw his commission disappearing. 'Kyrie Gaia lives in the mountains. Very beautiful place on top of a mountain. Very cool.' He grinned at Carla's pink face. 'Very beautiful, you must go there. Near Afionis.'

'Perhaps we could walk?'

'No,' he laughed, showing perfect teeth. 'Stavros will fix. Any other thing you want, ask Tetti, the maid in the taverna. She has a brother in Corfu who sells. He has a shop in Kerkira. Ask Tetti and she will tell Stavros and he–'

'He will fix,' said Carla. 'This Stavros, is he Mr Big in this village? Does he do it all? What about you, Iannis? Don't you ever make a quick buck?'

'Me?' His dark eyes were a study in

innocence. 'I do not buy or sell. Stavros does it. It is understood. I wait until a very rich lady comes and I marry her and go to America. My brother is there and he married a very rich wife with a restaurant.' He sighed. 'But I still wait. You are not rich?' He looked despondent.

'No,' said Samantha.

'Do we look rich?' said Carla.

'You do not look even as rich as me. It is good. We can be friends. I do not work hard this week. Petros helps in the taverna and I finish early tonight. I come to Maik's and you see me dance?'

'All for free?' Carla widened her eyes.

He shrugged. 'You buy a drink. I buy a drink. You watch me dance.' Carla pushed a packet of cigarettes over to him. 'It's a date,' she said.

'I toss you for coffee?' he said.

'No dice,' she said firmly.

'I like you,' he said. 'The woman in there I do not understand. She says I am a chimney... What is that?' He lit another cigarette from the stub of his old one. 'She says if she put a pot on my head, the smoke would come.' He shook his head. 'She says it many times and when I go now to take her coffee, she will say it again.'

'She means that you smoke too much, that's all.' Samantha turned to look once more at the sea. She caught her breath. Mr Gaia sat in the sun wearing a shirt and frayed shorts of a washed-out red that made his skin look even warmer, even darker. He sipped beer and seemed oblivious to anything but the letters he was reading. The tendons in his neck were tense and still as if carved in warm marble, the glowing hair untamed.

'He's quite beautiful,' said Carla.

'Spectacular,' said Samantha.

'I suppose he's the local stud with those good looks. No wonder he doesn't have to work for Stavros.'

'Who? Oh, you mean Iannis.'

'Who did you mean? Oh, I see. I do believe you are blushing. You haven't fallen for that inarticulate hunk of marble have you? If it's a holiday romance you want, better try for something easy that will be fun and over as soon as you leave here. Never chase the inaccessible, I've learned.' She sighed. 'A pity that all the talent is slinging food or hard to get.'

'I am *not* looking for that.'

'Sorry. Don't be mad at me, I was joking.'

'I don't even like that man,' went on Samantha, as if convincing herself. She stood up and picked up her bag. 'I want to get some sun cream before they close for the afternoon. See you back at the villa? I think I'll rest a little.'

She willed the man at the end table to go on reading, and wondered if her shorts hid the imprint of the cane and raffia chair that had dug into the bare flesh of her thighs, as she walked slowly past his table. The sea was empty of boats and there was no sign of the catamaran, but from the taverna balcony came a soft whining yawn. She looked up and saw the soft muzzle of the setter peeping between the bars. So they had come back from the sea another way. Eva had said that Mr Gaia went fishing with Stavros, so perhaps Stavros was entrusted with the catamaran.

'Wait for me. No harm in seeing what Stavros has in the way of cars, is there?' Carla panted after her. 'Prospero seems to, use the place as an office. He's on the phone now.'

They strolled past the shops, which were already shut against the mid-day heat, and on to the end of the village. The large concrete and iron garage backed on to the beach and a small landing stage. In the courtyard were three cars of fairly recent make, two of them clean and the other covered with a fine film of dust, but Samantha saw none of them. Her eyes were wide with incredulity as she stared at an old car, a real vintage car that had been carefully, lovingly restored, from its gleaming spoked wheels and shining paintwork to the leopard-skin upholstery and solid walnut fascia. A leather band encircled the long bonnet, and the hood was down to show pale beige leather linings. A jacket of cream linen had been thrown on the back seat.

'Stavros?' called Carla. 'Anyone at home?'

Samantha went forward, her fingers running along the shining coachwork. 'The Bugatti,' she murmured. But it wasn't possible. The old car that she remembered had been scratched and battered, with torn upholstery and dull metalwork.

She thought back to the day when she had gone into the barn behind the garage at home where her father and his team of mechanics made spare parts or repaired bits of the racing cars broken on the circuits. She was home from boarding school and her mother had died. It was the day after the funeral and her father was still red-eyed and sunk in grief. He had refused to talk to anyone and seemed to want even his daughter to go away, back to school, to leave him with his sorrow, never considering her own deep sense of loss and misery. The old car had stood under a sheet of plastic and she had climbed into it, feeling safe in the shabby interior, away from everyone who could hurt her. She leaned over the door and looked at the fascia. All old cars of the same type must be alike, but this one was special. Even if it wasn't the one in her father's garage, it was wonderful. Her pulse quickened. It would be thrilling to drive it. Even to sit in it just once would be enough to see if it gave her the same feeling as the other car gave her. She opened the door and sat in the driver's seat, her hands resting lightly on the huge wheel.

Carla gasped. 'Sam, what do you think you're doing?'

'It's beautiful. My father had one like it a long time ago.' She frowned, trying to force memories that refused to come out of the past. 'There was a man who wanted it and my father was having it restored. It was his hobby, restoring old cars, and the man came to see it.' She closed her eyes. The man came that day and found her in the car, weeping. He had lifted her up in his arms and carried her into the house to Mary, the housekeeper. He had strong arms and his curling hair had tickled her face, but she had only noticed his strength and gentleness; his face was blurred by her tears. She had gone back to school the next day and forgotten about the car, the man, and, in time, her tears.

Samantha climbed out of the car. 'Stavros isn't here. There's another man at the back who speaks no English, but Mr Big is away,' said Carla. They walked out on to the landing stage and saw the catamaran coming in under power.

'I thought Mr Gaia was in the taverna. He must move fast,' said Carla.

'I think that's Stavros,' said Samantha. The man tying the vessel to the quay was shorter and swarthier than the owner. As he jumped ashore carrying a bag of tools in his hand, Samantha murmured, 'I think Stavros has been fixing something.' Stavros smiled, showing the glint of gold fillings. 'Do you speak English?' asked Samantha.

'You want a car? Iannis said you would,' he said, with the satisfaction of one who knows he can read minds.

'How much?' asked Carla bluntly, and began to negotiate the hire of a car for six days.

'What about this one?' said Samantha, when the form had been signed.

Stavros laughed. 'You want that?' He seemed to find the idea of two women in the car a huge joke. 'You drive one like that in England?'

'Not quite like it, but near enough,' Samantha was goaded into replying. He raised a disbelieving eyebrow. Annoyed, she opened her bag and took out a photograph of her father, taken before his accident, smiling triumphantly into the camera with a huge trophy held high above his head, the car he had driven to win the race smoking gently in the background. 'My father – and he taught me to drive one rather like this for the London to Brighton run, if you've ever heard of it.'

'This is John Beachamp.' Stavros examined the picture with respect.

'You know about him?'

'Of course. He is famous,' he said simply.

'I'd like to look under the bonnet of the one we're hiring,' said Samantha firmly to hide the reluctant glow of pride.

'Then you take this one, not that,' said Stavros, dusting the sandy film from the dirty car. Under the bonnet the engine was clean and in good order. He grinned. 'This is better inside, but people choose the ones with no dust. Spiro!' The man from the back came out and Stavros spoke to him sharply. 'The car will be delivered with petrol and oil checked tomorrow morning,' he said. 'Spiro will do it tonight.'

'Well, whad-ya know?' said Carla. 'You're a dark horse, Sam. And I asked if you could drive!' She glanced back at the two men who were watching them leave. 'But who would have thought Stavros could keep a car like that. It's worth a fortune.'

'Might have no engine,' said Samantha. 'A lot of vintage cars are kept for show and he might do a brisk trade in photography. You know the thing: sit in a vintage car and have a period photograph taken.' She was puzzled. 'It looks too good for that, and come to think of it, the bonnet over the engine was warm. It's been driven recently.'

'We'd better move if we're to bathe before dinner. What do you say to a trip into Corfu, or Kerkira as Eva calls it?'

'Good idea. I want to take some snaps of some of the wayside shrines we saw on the way from the airport. I can buy some more clothes, too. I'm just about ready to throw away practically everything I brought with me.'

'Well, don't go mad just because one hunk of man eyes you when you go by.'

'Iannis? Oh, really! He couldn't look at any woman in any other way. It's all part of his work.'

'I wasn't thinking about Iannis,' said

Carla, and closed her bedroom door.

Her skin glowed and Samantha covered herself with fragrant after-sun lotion when she was dry. It was pleasurable to feel the sunkissed warmth of her skin, to brush out the cloud of dark hair and to slip into the pale dress again. The cotton dress showed off her deepening tan in almost sharp relief and her eyes looked huge and very blue, as if they had been washed by the colour of the sea.

Carla was waiting in a long-sleeved silk shirt to cover the redness of her arms, but the pale blue made her blonde prettiness apparent.

'Do you see what I see?' said Carla. 'Two new arrivals. Um... Which do you fancy?'

'Neither. How many times do I have to tell you that I am here to get away from wolves?'

'They don't look like wolves to me.' Carla sat at their usual table and Sam was amused to see that she didn't take the coveted seat with the view of the sea, but sat facing the other diners. The sky was clear but for tiny wisps of cloud that hovered like slivers of mother-of-pearl glowing pale pink and gold against the turquoise sky. The sea merged with the horizon into infinite pallor, but was dark near the shore, and the headland glowed as if a fire had been lit to send it into relief.

Eva floated by. 'You like our sunset?'

'You shouldn't have ordered it just for us,' said Samantha. Eva shook with laughter. 'It's beautiful,' said the girl with flowing dark hair and glowing eyes who looked so different tonight.

'It is good for love. Very good for love,' said Eva. She brought a bottle of wine and poured some into three glasses. She raised her glass and the girls did the same. 'Yammass!' she said.

'Yammass,' said Carla, and looked at the fair-haired boy who had arrived that day and was still city-pale.

The food arrived and they ate grilled red mullet and stuffed aubergines, and more delicious bread than anyone watching their diet would dare to eat, and followed it with black coffee and baklava, the honey-soaked almond pastry that is so good with the bitter coffee but too sweet for some people eaten on its own. The wine was light and dry and as the sunset faded into blue-black night, the stars came out and the music from Maik's Café Alcinous came down the street.

'We'd better go now and get a table,' said Carla. 'I think I saw some people from the hotel over the other side of the bay looking in the windows. We can't have foreigners taking over!'

'How insular can you get? A few days here and you are a true Corfiot.' Samantha glanced up at the balcony and her pulse quickened. The windows were flung wide and a light glowed in the bedroom. Shadows flitted as a man walked about the room, and then the light was switched off. Surely he wasn't going to bed already? Perhaps the night out fishing had exhausted even the wonderful Mr Gaia.

Samantha followed Carla and found her already sitting at one of the best tables, but noticed that there was room for six more people. 'I thought you didn't want to mix with the hotel crowd. Why not have a table for two or even four?' Samantha sighed. 'Oh, I get it.'

The two men they had seen in the taverna hesitated at the door, saw Carla laughing and went in. They looked round and spoke to Hebe, Maik's wife. She smiled and waved a hand as if to say they could sit anywhere. Carla smiled and the men stopped at the table.

'Do you mind? This is our first visit and we don't know our way around,' said the fair-haired man. 'I'm Brendan Cary and this is Ben Mathers.' His shy smile gave lie to his direct approach and, in spite of her inner resistance, Samantha liked them. Carla made the necessary introductions and the men followed their example and ordered ouzo, which arrived with the usual accompaniment of glasses of cool water and a large dish of mehzedes, the appetisers offered in many cafés to be eaten with ouzo.

Carla nibbled a shrimp as if she was still hungry and Samantha piled taramasalata on to a small cracker. 'This is good,' she said.

'Are you staying at the taverna?' asked Brendan. 'We have a holiday apartment in one of the villas at the back of the village. No sea view, but okay.'

Carla told them about the villa. The café filled up quickly. The first sirtaki of the evening was in progress when Iannis arrived and came to the table. He put a packet of cigarettes on the table and called for ouzo. Brendan looked annoyed and Samantha stifled a smile. He's attracted to Carla and thinks she's got something going with the waiter, she thought.

'You told us you were coming here to dance... Well, what are you waiting for?' Carla challenged him. 'Can't you see we've come specially to cheer you on?' Brendan's face cleared as Iannis joined the dancers.

Evening became night and the dancing grew more frenetic as one after another of the local men tried their skill and visitors were dragged, laughing, to join in.

Samantha resisted when Iannis pulled her to her feet, but gave in with a shrug when Ben said he wanted to dance and needed her moral support. The stylised movements took all their attention and Samantha became absorbed in the strange but compelling dance. She watched her feet and the feet of the expert Greek dancer by her side. He seemed able to flow with the music and yet make the abrupt semi-stops required with perfect control. The music stopped and she joined the clapping for more, but the floor was cleared.

More ouzo had arrived, with a large dish of Greek salad and more pieces of fried squid and shrimps. 'I thought we'd be hungry after all that so I ordered it,' said Carla.

'Do you always eat as much as this?' asked Brendan.

'I had a deprived childhood,' she said, and they smiled as if they already shared a deep rapport. Samantha felt suddenly lonely. The music was playing softly, the atmosphere was good, but her heart was empty. How easy it was for Carla to make friends with men and take it lightly. Her heart ached for her loss of trust in men after the experiences she had suffered at the hands of guests in her father's house. It was difficult to believe that Brendan and Ben would be the same, but she now knew that men were beasts with smooth talk and lust in their hearts.

She looked across the room at the dark heads of the Greeks and the lighter-coloured skin and hair of the majority of the visitors, and pushed back a tress of her own dark hair. I look more like them than any of the visitors, she thought. What had Eva said? You look like the Princess Nausicaa. 'Who was Nausicaa?' she said to Iannis, who sank into the seat opposite.

He looked at her blankly, and Ben laughed. 'Never ask a local. They have no pride in their own history or myths.'

'And you know, I suppose?'

'That's why I'm here. I want to spend at least two days in the museum of Kerkira. I'm a historian and I'm writing a book about the links between Shakespeare, Kerkira and Homer.'

'I know about Prospero and Miranda and Ariel,' said Samantha, slowly, 'but I know nothing about Homer.'

'Odysseus sailed from Ithaka for the Trojan wars and on his way back had many adventures. Briefly, he was shipwrecked on an island which we think was Kerkira, and the Princess Nausicaa found him naked and bruised on the shore. She was the only one not to run away and she covered him with blankets and had him carried to her father's Alcinous' palace.'

'It's fascinating,' said Samantha, her eyes shining. 'So Prospero was an idea taken from the ancient Greek?'

'And we've already seen Prospero,' said Carla. 'Come to think, Odysseus suits him too. The kind of man who would leave his wife for a tiny matter of a war and take his time getting back home. He'd expect her to be waiting, doing that grotty bit of tapestry for years. You see, I know my Homer too.'

'Not quite as I'd put it,' said Ben dryly, 'but it gives the picture.'

'But you must admit he does look the part – rather shattering.'

'Who are we talking about?' asked Ben patiently.

'He's over there talking to Stavros and tucking into souvlaki as if there was no tomorrow.'

Samantha turned and saw Mr Gaia through a mist of smoke. He was laughing, and for the first time she saw the true humour and ease of manner that must exist in any man who loved animals. She was fascinated by the set of his head crowned with the riot of dark auburn curls, and in profile he was like an aristocratic cameo. A laurel wreath would complete the picture, she thought with quickening breath, and tried to tear her gaze away. As if sensing another mind touching his own, Gaia turned and saw her bright eyes and parted lips. For a long moment they were locked in a capsule of communication that needed no words, no physical contact, but from it a tiny flame flickered, gathered strength and settled into something beyond their control. It was hidden memory that both knew lay in the dusty corners of their minds... But where had they met?

Samantha lowered her eyes first. It would always be so, she thought. His arrogant gaze would dominate anyone, male or female; he would take what he wanted of life, of success, of women. She shuddered. If he wanted a woman, could any woman resist him?

'He has a fine boat,' said Iannis hating to be left out of the conversation but understanding little of what was being said.

'He has a catamaran,' said Carla. 'It's great! I've known one or two but this one beats everything.'

'What's it called?' asked Ben.

'An English name. He has many things English. His dog he talks to in English because it came from your country and like you does not understand Greek!'

'The catamaran?'

'Oh, yes. He calls it *The Flying Turtle*,' said Iannis

'Turtles again,' said Carla. 'Show Ben your coin, Sam.'

'My father gave it to me as a good luck charm.' She took it from her handbag and Ben came closer to examine it. The fair head and the dark were touching, and from across the room, it looked as if the man and woman who had only just met were very intimate indeed. Gaia stared and his brow darkened, and when Samantha looked up he was watching her with a look of sardonic rejection, as if she was making a quick pick-up from the latest arrivals.

'Just who does he think he is,' she said crossly.

Iannis glanced at him and back to

Samantha and smiled, glad to give information. 'You do not know his name? He is Rhexenor Gaia, who owns many many olive trees.'

3

'And did you buy many pretty things in Kerkira?' Eva beamed and lowered herself into a chair under the awning. Petros brought iced tea and set the tray down on the table. Samantha stretched lazily in the sun and reached up for the cold glass that Eva handed to her. The brief bikini showed off her deepening tan, and the brilliant scarlet of the tiny garments seemed less bright than when she had bought them and wondered if red wasn't too garish even for the beach.

'I bought two more dresses and some cotton trousers and an embroidered shirt. Oh yes, and some sandals and a straw hat in case the sun is too strong even for me.'

'And I bought a huge hat and loads of suncream,' said Carla glumly from her seat in the shade. 'I shouldn't have dried off in the sun after our swim this morning, but at least the salt water convinced me, that I should have my hair cut short.' She ran her fingers through the light, fair curls. 'I shall keep out of the sun for a day to let my skin harden off.'

The catamaran was at its mooring and Samantha eyed it with curiosity. There was no sign of its owner and yet she sensed that he was near. She lay out on a sun-lounger on the sand and put her sun-glasses on the towel at her side. The red ribbon that she had stuffed in the pocket of her shorts when she left the beach the day before had gone and her hair needed something to keep it from her eyes. The dinghy was beached, so it seemed unlikely that Rhexenor Gaia was on the boat. She closed her eyes. Rhexenor... It suited him. It had a ring of elegance and force. Was he ever called Rhex for short? Rhex... She had heard the name in England, but at the garage there were few men's names that she hadn't heard. The constant flow of customers and visitors to the famous ex-racing driver left a blur of faces and names which she had no desire to recall.

A wet tongue on her arm made her start, and she looked up into the amiable mask of the red setter at a level with her own face.

'Ariel, you beautiful dog,' she said, and rubbed him behind the ears. He wagged his tail and lay on the sand with his face on her bare knees. He gazed up soulfully. Then Samantha heard the crunch of pebbles as Rhexenor Gaia jumped down to the beach. She continued to rub the dog's ears.

'Ariel, come here!' The dog ignored him. 'Ariel!' The voice was sharper, as if unused to being disobeyed. The tail flickered and Ariel turned his head to look at his master, but any other movement was slight. One or two people drinking at the tables under the awning looked to see what was happening, and as Rhexenor Gaia came towards Samantha, she saw his annoyed embarrassment. She was acutely aware of him. His body was golden brown and his feet were bare and well-shaped. His shorts were only fractionally more respectable than the frayed ones he had worn the previous day, and they clung to his body, soaking from the sea.

'Ariel, you are a bad dog,' he said. The dog wagged his tail and stayed where he was comfortable, his tongue out, panting slightly. Rhexenor Gaia half smiled, politely, and put out a hand to take the dog. He grasped him by the ear, but the fur was slippery and wet and Ariel slithered away, closer to Samantha, like a wet seal. He was now on his knees, inches away from her, and she could smell the scent of salt and sun on a male body. His eyes seemed to strip her of the vestigial clothes she wore and she instinctively put a hand to cover her bosom. He bent forward and plucked the dog into his arms, and as his arm brushed against hers, a current of shock sped from his touch to the inmost chambers of her heart. He froze for an instant – because he felt the same reaction? Samantha wondered. Or just to gain his balance before standing erect with the dog over his shoulder like a bag of molasses?

'I'm sorry, he has no manners,' he said. 'But it isn't wise to encourage strange dogs.'

'He came to me,' said Samantha. 'I didn't encourage him.'

'I wonder why?' The smile was fleeting and arrogant. 'You must have something more than your more obvious attractions. He doesn't go to strangers.' He looked at her red bikini and his eyes were angry. He fumbled in one pocket with difficulty as Ariel still lay across his shoulders like a dead sheep. 'Is this yours?'

Samantha saw her crumpled hair ribbon in his brown hand. 'Yes. I wondered where it was.'

'Spiro found it inside my car. He also said that you were in the garage hiring a car, so I assume this is yours. Please remember that the hire cars are none of my business but the Bugatti is my concern and my concern alone. I do not allow tourists to invade my privacy!'

'The Bugatti is your car?'

'Of course. Who could own a car like that but me?'

'I imagine a great many people could do so,' she said, her temper rising. 'It isn't only men with more money than sense who buy them. There are people who restore them with love and make them priceless and can't bear to part with them even if they almost ruin themselves by keeping them.' She glared at him, her breasts rising and falling in her agitation. The tension between them burst into a flame of anger.

'Well, just remember, I allow no other person to step inside that car.' He threw the ribbon on the sand, where it unravelled like a stream of blood. Shakily, she picked it up and screwed it into a ball, then smoothed it out and rolled it neatly and put it carefully with the turtle coin in her bag.

'The Kyrie has gone?' Eva turned back and called to Petros to take the tray to the room with the balcony. 'I saw you talking with him. He is very beautiful, yes?' Eva gave a sly grin.

'If you like that type,' said Samantha shortly. 'I was talking to the dog. He has better manners than his master.'

'He is nice big man, very good, very handsome. Many women ask about him. but he does not eat here unless it is in the room up there.'

'He thinks he's too good for your guests, Eva.'

'No, he is a private man. But you say you talked to the dog. The so silly name, but it has to be when the dog understands no Greek. He takes no notice of me.'

'He came when I called,' said Samantha.

'That is good. You are fortunate. You may call and the man may come also.'

'Don't be absurd,' said Samantha, her colour rising, Eva gave a knowing wink. 'You don't think I made friends with the dog so that I could get to know that awful man, do you? I know nothing about him, but I have met men of his kind – self-opinionated and imagining that they can take anything they want.'

'You must know very handsome men,' said Eva dryly. 'But I will tell you about him.' She settled herself on the protesting chair. 'You have seen his boat, *The Flying Turtle*. Even that name is English. He leaves it with Stavros when he goes home to his mountain, and Stavros uses it to go fishing and to take tourists.'

'So there *are* things he doesn't mind sharing – at a price,' murmured Samantha.

'Kyrie Gala has a fine house.' Eva stretched her arms wide. 'He has many, many olive trees,' she said in a hushed voice. 'He has cars and servants and many many business, but he likes to come here alone with his dog.'

'And Mrs Gaia? What does she do while he is swanning off? Does she like sailing?' asked Carla, with a slightly mocking smile.

'There is no wife. She died two years ago. She was on the mountain and fell from her horse. The Kyrie was in Athens and did not know until he returned to find police at his house. He no longer dances in the cafés with his friends and he is silent too much. He needs love.'

'Surely he can solve that, even on a temporary basis,' said Carla.

Eva was shocked. 'There are many who would share his bed but he does not want. There are those who try to reach his heart, but he has no heart – only for a dog!' She gave an impatient thump to the table. 'A dog, when he is so beautiful and still young.'

She stopped as Rhexenor Gaia strode from the taverna, his hand gripping the dog's collar firmly as he went down to the sea. The dog jumped into the inflatable, and within two minutes the dinghy was tied to the stern of the catamaran. Samantha watched with an unexplained ache in her heart. He could be Prospero, or Odysseus setting out to sail away across the Aegean Sea. The man on deck stood with feet apart, his muscular shoulders braced to raise the sail as the mild air took it. The bright blue sail billowed softly and the rust-red dog danced out of the way to stand like a figurehead with the breeze combing his ears.

'Quite, quite beautiful,' said Carla softly. 'How did Homer put it? "And grey-eyed Athena sent him a favourable gale ... singing over the wine-dark sea." And now I know it to be true.'

'I've sand in my pants,' said Samantha. 'I think I'll shower and dress in something more suitable for this evening. Are the two men coming back in time for dinner?'

'Interested, in spite of what you said?'

'No, but after *that* man, anyone would be acceptable for an evening's conversation!'

'Ouch! He has a talent for rubbing you up the wrong way.'

'It seems to be mutual,' said Samantha. 'If we're with the others it will pass the time,' she finished lamely. She could not explain that when Rhexenor Gaia was there she felt vulnerable, as if some force more powerful than any that had touched her life drew her to him whether she wanted it or not, and she knew that he despised her. She took out the red ribbon to wash it, and as it fell into the hot soapy water, the scent of his body was there with her, invading her chaste pale room with his maleness.

'Can you come in?' shouted Carla. 'Can you put some cream on my back?'

'It's very red,' said Samantha. 'I'll be as gentle as I can, but you'll have to go easily for a day or so.'

'I think I'll stay here tomorrow and write cards and stay in the shade. It's no hardship and I ought to write home. Will you find something to do?'

'Of course. I still haven't taken any photographs of those shrines. I might use the car and explore.'

They went down to dinner, and when Brendan and Carla met, they laughed. One pink face looked at the other. 'Snap!' said Carla. 'But I bet my back is more sore than yours.'

'Let's compare later,' he said with a wicked grin, and she gave him a dirty look. 'All right, sorry. Anything, if you'll promise not to touch my sunburn.'

'We seem the toughest ones here, Samantha,' said Ben. 'I love the sun. But I forgot just how hot it was in the café in the square in Kerkira. I left poor old Brendan frying while I was in the museum, and the bus was stifling on the way back.'

'You went by bus? I thought you were hiring a Stavros special?'

'Not a hope. He is all booked up for days.' He hesitated. 'I suppose you aren't going into Kerkira again? Or could I pay for a day's hire and have the car when you aren't using it?'

'I wasn't planning to go in so soon, but Carla is staying here tomorrow to get rid of her sunburn, so I could drive you in, have a look at the coins you told me were like my turtle coin and take some photographs. We could arrange to meet up again and be back in time for a meal.'

'That's great. Are you sure you don't mind? Do you feel like another jaunt, Brendan?'

'Not if I can avoid it. I'm staying here tomorrow. I shall drink all the cold beer in the place and anoint myself with sun oil – in the shade.' And Samantha saw that even the discomfort of sunburn wouldn't stop them enjoying a day together. She smiled slyly at Carla, who blushed.

'Greek salad is good for everything, including sunburn,' said Ben. 'Let's get dinner over and go to Maik's. I want to record some of the music, and he said that there would be two real bouzouki players who know some of the older tunes. I already have some on tape, but there must be many that might get forgotten after a couple more generations if the young men don't play them.'

Samantha felt safe now that the catamaran was out of sight, with the disturbing man on board. Perhaps he can get to his side of the island and his mountain from the headland

and won't be with us in the café tonight, she thought, and made up her mind that she would enjoy the simple pleasures of music and light-hearted company.

They were greeted as if they were old friends and Maik made a great show of offering them a really good selection of tit-bits to eat with their ouzo or metaxa. One or two of the young men danced to the cassettes of Greek music, but the bouzouki players didn't put in an appearance until very late. A buzz went round the café as an old man sat in the space for dancing and sang a long saga of ancient battles, triumphs and tragedy, his face lined and hardened by sun and wind, his eyes still keen and his voice having a quality of sincerity that made up for lack of artistry. Ben took it all down on tape and grew excited. Revived by a tumbler of dark retsina and a handful of olives, the old man sang again, and it was obvious that everyone held him in great respect. Even the more brash young men sat and listened, their dark eyes full of handed-down folk memory and their restless feet still.

Ben left the table to join the bouzouki players and was soon in close conversation with the old man.

'I didn't realise how much Greek he knew,' said Carla. 'Brendan did say that he was a bit of an egghead, but I confess I'm very impressed.' Samantha glanced round at the eager laughing faces and smiled when she thought how unlike an evening in a pub at home this scene was.

Samantha saw two men stop in the crowded doorway and her heart faltered. Rhexenor Gaia swept the room with an imperious glance and Maik pushed through the throng and said something to four men who were not buying drinks but sitting playing cards. They muttered angrily, but left their seats and sat at a table outside the café, under the awning used during the day for shade. The light from the curtainless windows gave them light enough for playing and left a free table, which Mr Gaia accepted as his right.

'Does he own the place?' whispered Carla. Samantha shook her head. She had a feeling that anything they said could be heard at the next table, where he was now sitting. She pretended to be interested in the music players, and Ben came back and began an involved account of the origins of the piece being played. He bent close to make himself heard as, his voice was soft, and once more there seemed to be a bond of intimacy between the serious-eyed man and the girl with the blue-grey eyes.

The music changed and a sigh went through the café. 'It's the table dance,' said Ben. 'Excuse me, I want to get the music without too much interference.' He picked up his tape recorder and went back to the players, leaving a gap through which Samantha couldn't avoid seeing Rhexenor Gaia. He glanced at her, and for a moment seemed about to speak, then he smiled to himself, turned to Stavros and spoke to him, and Samantha felt that he was talking about her. She looked towards the dance floor.

'There are two men who dance this dance. I cannot,' said Iannis, with regret. 'Petros is good and he may come here later, but I think we shall have to listen only.'

'What about the other one? You said there were two.'

He looked embarrassed, and she saw that Rhexenor Gaia was listening with a deep frown on his face. 'I do not know. I mean only Petros,' he said.

'If there is someone, can't he be persuaded? It seems a pity that the musicians have bothered to come – you said from the other side of the island, didn't you? They must feel insulted if nobody dances to their music.'

Iannis gave a half frightened look towards the man staring at them and turned to call for more metaxa. Maik came to the table with the bottle and nodded to Mr Gaia, speaking in rapid Greek. He sounded sad and glanced wistfully towards the musicians. 'What did he say?' whispered Carla.

Ben came back and there was no need for Iannis to speak. 'It's a crying shame,' he said. 'They can play this music and there is no one to dance to it. They say that there is a man who is expert but he gave it up long ago.'

'Is he here? It must be one of the old men. There must come a time when they run out of puff,' said Samantha. 'From what I've seen, they love showing off far too much to give up unless they're really past it.'

A gasp from Iannis told her that she had said something wrong. A sudden movement from the next table also told her that Rhexenor Gaia had heard every word and didn't like it one bit! He stood before her, with a mocking smile on his lips. His eyes flashed blue fire and his body was tense in every line.

'I will show you, Miss Beauchamp. I will show you that it is by choice that I do not dance, not because I am past it.' The fury and offended pride made him truly formidable as he strode to the clear space between the tables. 'Maik, I dance!' he said.

There was a scurry as Maik and Stavros selected a square café table and put it at one end of the room and arranged chairs in a certain pattern to keep the dance space clear. Samantha sat as if turned to stone, her heightened colour adding to the glow of her sun-kissed skin. He knows my name, she thought. He was told it by Stavros when he found my ribbon. Her heart beat madly. And he remembered it. He disliked me so much over that stupid little incident that my name stuck in his mind. A secret smile made the corners of her lips twitch. I may have insulted him, but at least he knows now that I exist and I'm not just a being in a dull green dress, far beneath his notice.

The music began slowly, with the solitary dancer going through the languorous introduction, his skill making it seem flowing and effortless but bringing sharp sighs from the watching Greeks. An accompaniment of slow hand-clapping emphasised the beat, and the throb of the ancient musical instruments told a tale as old as time. Samantha watched, and every other person in the room seemed to vanish into a mist. There was one man, dancing with all the control and skill of a ballet dancer, with the abandonment and passion of a satyr, with the desperation of a man who had almost forgotten life and love and who found the reawakening within the framework of the dance an experience of wonder and pain. There was this one man and one woman in the room. She knew the bond was of her making and that he felt only dislike and anger towards her. But at least they were positive emotions to meet and match hers. As she watched, she knew that her bond was not born of hate. She sensed the eroticism of the dance and yet could find no revulsion towards him, only a reluctant tenderness, as if she needed to fill something in his emptiness as well as her own.

He took the table by one leg and danced,

his body arching close to the ground. The crowd called encouragement and the watching faces showed more signs of tension than the now expressionless face of the dancer lost in his ritual. It was a mask of copper, fringed with an amber glow. He put down the table and slowly, still dancing, unbuttoned his silk shirt. At each turn, nearly on his knees, then stretching tall, another button was released to expose the fine silky hairs on his broad chest. Another and another, and he slipped his arms from the sleeves, brandishing the light fluid garment that seemed alive, so that it rose and fell like a veil, the ochre silk following a question mark in the air.

He turned and seemed to hover between floor and air, looking straight into the wide grey-blue eyes of the girl who had dared to challenge him. The silk shirt came in a gentle stream and landed softly on her lap. He turned away and seized the table again, dancing with intricate steps and tense muscles. He held it high by one leg and then held the corner of the table in his teeth. Round and round the floor he danced, the table held only by his mouth. He banged on the table and Maik put glasses and plates on it until Carla gave a cry of apprehension. The dancing stopped, the table was placed gently on the floor as if it were as light as goosedown, and Rhexenor Gaia seemed to come to life.

Samantha held out the shirt to him and he came to her slowly. He seized her hand and pulled her to her feet, his eyes gleaming with malice and something that stirred her unwilling heart. He shouted, and the music began again – a rapid beat that sent people on to the floor, dancing in a line, hands on the waists of the person in front, until twenty – thirty – forty people snaked round the room and out into the warm blackness. They danced along the quayside, where the only light came from the stars and the glinted reflections of lamps from balconies. The fragrance of herbs growing behind the villas and the smells from the dying barbecue pit behind the kitchen were of Greece and no other place on earth. The hands that spanned her small waist held her as if he had made her his prisoner, and she felt an alien rush of excitement smothering her inhibitions.

The line danced back, breathlessly, and at the door he drew her into the shadows. 'My shirt?'

He had flung it round her neck, tying the sleeves to keep them firm as they began the dance. He untied the sleeves, slowly because the knot was tight, and all the time Samantha had an overwhelming awareness of a rapid pulse beat in his throat. He slid the silk from her shoulders and gazed down at her, his eyes blank.

'You danced beautifully...' She faltered.

'So I am not past it?'

She shook her head.

'Because a man chooses to deny himself many things that he could take means nothing but that it is his choice to wait.' He took her shoulders in his hands and his mouth came hard against her lips. She saw the dark eyes gleam with the wicked light of the satyr she had watched dancing and smelled the earthy tang that must have followed defenceless maidens in the days of the god Pan. It was wonderful and terrible and she drew away ashamed of her weakness in responding to his kiss.

She fled back to the safety of the café, to bright lights and dancing men, and coffee – instead of the elixir of the gods.

'Where is he? I must talk to him,' said Ben.

'I don't know. I only danced with him,' said Samantha unsteadily.

'Is that all?' said Carla. 'Pity he took his shirt back. I'd like one like it.' She considered Samantha's pink cheeks. 'Touch of the sun? Or touch of the moon?'

'Neither,' said Samantha, 'I'm just hot. I wonder if Maik has some really cold orange juice.' She glanced towards the door and saw that Rhexenor Gaia was talking to the men playing cards outside. She sipped her orange juice and looked again, but he had gone. When they left the café, he was still nowhere to be seen.

Lights shone in the garage through chinks in the closed metal doors and there was no light from the room with the balcony. 'That was a good evening,' said Carla, turning to look back at Brendan and Ben, who were walking through the village to their own apartment.

'You should get on well tomorrow, too. Brendan seems likely to become your shadow,' said Samantha. She wanted to talk of other things, to thrust away all thoughts of the evening, the dancing and the man who threatened to change her life. I must put him out of my mind; he's like a disease and I must fight my own feelings if I'm to go home and be content, she decided. 'I'm getting up early so that Ben can have at least four hours in the museum. Anything you want me to get for you while I'm in Corfu town?'

They reached the villa and climbed the

stairs. 'You could get more film and another pair of sunglasses like the ones I bought – I sat on the others.'

'Any plans for tomorrow?'

'I'm taking Brendan to feed the turtles. Very interested in turtles, he is. And I can read a good book, if there's nothing to do.' She giggled. 'He thinks I'm on a longed-for holiday for which I had to save up for two. years.'

'So what?'

'He gets all protective and buys all my drinks.'

'That's not like you, Carla. You've plenty of money.'

'Yes, I know. But don't tell him. This is the first time I've had a man interested who isn't after my money.' She paused at the blue door. 'Promise you won't tell. It might be important.' She went into her room and closed the door behind her.

'Well, well,' said Samantha. She went to the window and leaned out over the sea. Once more she felt a lingering sadness.

Lucky Carla, with someone who was rapidly falling in love with her.

The empty sea lay trembling beneath the stars and the music had stopped. A slight splashing made her turn her head towards the shore. She heard footsteps on the shingle at the edge of the beach, a deep warm voice calling a dog and the answering bark from the path to the headland.

4

Samantha locked the car and squinted up at the sun, trying to think of the best place to leave the car for some hours, but there was very little shade anywhere in the car park and she just hoped that Stavros bought good tyres for his hired cars.

'Will this do?' she asked.

'Fine. It's very good of you to drive all this way again, but it's far more comfortable than waiting for crowded buses. When you've finished shopping or whatever you want to do here, come into the museum and find me and I'll show you the coin collection,' said Ben.

He gave her directions and she smiled goodbye. It was pleasant to have company sometimes, but her heart lifted at the thought of a whole morning on her own, roaming the quaint back-streets of the fascinating town, pleasing herself and taking photographs when anything interesting took her attention.

She walked under the lofty gloom of the Italianate arcades and went down tiny side-streets whose shops were hung with every possible kind of souvenir and hundreds of beautiful skirts and dresses, blouses and kaftans. There were piles of thick woollen sweaters and knitted coats, indicating the winter task of the women of Corfu, who sat making them during the wet season, using home-spun wool from the local sheep and goats and blending shades of grey and black with the natural cream fibres in a way that was simple and yet smart. It was too warm to think of buying anything made of thick wool, but she found delight in spending more of the generous sum that her father had insisted on giving her. The cool cottons were irresistible and she added two more strap-topped dresses to her growing ward-robe. A window full of silk shirts in glowing colours brought her wanderings to a pause. The ochre silk was exactly like the one she had felt, like a caress, round her neck while the wild dance took her out into the warm Corfiot night, with the man who fascinated her holding her waist with his strong, unforgettable hands, and taking the shirt back with a kiss that was half passion and half insult.

She tore herself away and bought the films that Carla wanted and some more for her own camera. The horse-drawn carriages in line by the square made a charming picture, as each horse nodded under a straw flower-decked bonnet through which its ears twitched lazily. The background of purple bougainvillaea made a background of dramatic impact.

Samantha wandered further down towards the sea. The air was filled with the scent of flowering shrubs, which surrounded the main square and the cricket pitch, and she sat for a while, sipping a cool drink under the bright awning of a café overlooking the old harbour.

An ancient garrison, still manned by soldiers, made a gaunt contrast with the flowers, and she watched a group of children swimming in a sheltered cove. Then she bought a guide book and wondered if the Church of Foreigners would be near the museum. She sighed, suddenly wanting company, and went to find Ben.

A white ferry boat was docking and Samantha stopped to look at the passengers come down the steep gangplank. Women in black came down, bent under huge loads of cases and bundles; smart tourists with well-cut clothes and light hand luggage; and students in grubby jeans, back-packing and seeing paradise for perhaps the last time before they settled to full-time employment and the restrictions of adult life.

Samantha drew back into the shade of an overgrown bush and watched a man stride forward to greet a beautiful Greek woman, who smiled and put up her face to be kissed.

The muted elegance of the slim woman put her apart from every other passenger as she allowed Rhexenor Gaia to take her two cases and precede her to a car that Samantha had not noticed, gleaming under a shady tree. With a hand lightly on his shoulder, the woman took her place in the Bugatti and Rhexenor Gaia turned to say something to her that made her laugh up into his animated face. The girl who watched from the shadows saw them through a haze of incredulity. He wasn't interested in women, or so Eva said. He showed how much he despised the needs of the flesh by his insolent kiss and then complete rejection, and yet he was with a woman who looked into his eyes with love and he smiled.

With a hollow sense of loss, Samantha went to the museum, trying to put the couple from her mind. It was stupid to feel so deeply about a man who had done nothing but insult or deride her since she first saw him. It would be even more stupid to fall in love with him. But the warning bells rang in her mind, too late, and she knew that for the first time in her life, she was jealous of another woman.

'The coins are on this floor,' said Ben, glad to be of use to the pretty girl who was becoming an increasingly important part of his holiday. Samantha forced a smile. They examined the case of ancient coins and she asked intelligent questions, but she wasn't aware of the answers.

They lunched on salad and ice cream and sipped coffee overlooking the port.

'They say that if you sit and watch boats long enough, you are sure to see someone you know,' said Ben, laughing.

'Is that so?' said Samantha. 'I wonder who you'll see?'

'I can't think of anyone I want to see, except you,' he said, and turned slightly pink.

Please don't fall in love with me, she willed him. It would be sensible for me to love someone like you, but how can I settle for embers when a flame threatens to engulf me? She smiled and talked of the shrines she had yet to photograph, and, eager to please, he suggested that they look quickly at anything she wanted to be shown in Kerkira and then concentrate on the shrines, of which there were many varieties. He took her to the Church of Foreigners and explained its history, and in spite of herself, Samantha was interested.

'I won't bore you with too much detail,' he said. 'The church contains the relics of the patron saint of Kerkira – St Spirodon – but the church is called St Nikolaos of Foreigners. The relics have been there since the early sixteenth century, but the poor old saint had a rough passage before that. He was actually born in Cyprus. Do you want some more culture?'

'If it means being in the cool, yes, please.'

'Well the church walls are thick enough and we can look round until the heat slackens.'

The interior was blue and white and silent. Tapers burned in ornate silver holders on gold stands and several women bent in prayer, black head-scarves shrouding their lined faces.

'I think we'd better go,' whispered Samantha. 'I feel out of place with my head uncovered. I'll bring a head-scarf if I come again.'

They walked slowly back to the car and left the doors open for a few minutes to avoid being roasted as soon as they sat in it. 'Soon be cool if we set up our own breeze,' she said. They stopped at intervals to take pictures of the tiny well-kept shrines that dotted the roadside, each with its white cross stark against the green bank or the blue sky.

'Most of them are dedicated to St Spiro and most of the male children are still called after him, which can be a little confusing. If you want something and call for Spiro, you'll have at least three coming to see what you want,' said Ben. 'Do you realise what the time is? It's a long drive back and we seem to have wandered off the main road. I wonder if there's a taverna in that village I can see through the trees on the side of the hill?'

'But you want to get back...'

'No, nothing would give me greater pleasure than to take you to dinner. It's the least I can do after your kindness and your company.'

'We'll drive up to the village and if there's a good taverna we'll stay, but if it means going any further, I think we should go back.'

'Agreed.'

They drove in silence, enjoying the calm of the side-road and the lazy music of the cicadas in the trees. The road opened out and they found a wide flagstoned courtyard backed by an old taverna with tables on a terrace under the vines.

'This looks good,' said Ben, and they left the car just off the road in the shade.

'I wonder what the others are doing,' said

Samantha, to fill the silence when they had ordered aperitifs.

'Not sunbathing!' said Ben. 'Come on, the proprietor is beckoning us to choose what we want for our dinner.'

They went into the spotless kitchen and the cook lifted one lid after another to show them what was on the menu. Samantha chose lamb souvlaki, while Ben decided on lamb cooked with herbs and tomatoes, Greek salad and dolmades, the tight little parcels of spiced rice and meat wrapped in vine leaves. He chose the wine carefully and Samantha was aware that he knew much more about the country than the usual tourist.

'Ask him what is further up the hill, Ben.'

Ben spoke to the man in Greek and they talked for a few minutes, with much gesticulation on the Greek's part.

'He says it leads to the mountains and then to a very pretty bay on the other side of the island. The island is narrow here and it isn't far to the sea on the other side. He also said that there is a village at the top called Afionis, quite a beauty spot, according to him.'

'Afionis? I've heard that word somewhere. Is there a coach trip there?'

'No, it's private land, but walkers are allowed there. It's all owned by one man. As Eva says, he owns many many olive trees – which is the Greek way of measuring wealth. The land passes from one generation to the next and the olive trees are as ancient as time. They make the bond that ties families to the land, as they represent a responsibility that has to be served.'

'And the man who owns it?' She had no need to ask.

'Rhexenor Gaia, the man who danced the table dance. Now if only I could get to know him, I think I might discover a lot about the culture of this island. With a wealthy family that goes back as far as his there must be wonderful records and a great deal of handed-down folk lore. I wonder...' He looked at Samantha speculatively.

'Well, I wish you luck,' she said. 'I have met him, but I wouldn't recommend it. He's an arrogant bore.'

He smiled. 'I'm glad you think so, Samantha. He struck me as the type that women fall for, and I'm relieved to know that he doesn't impress you.' He took her hand across the table and gazed at her. 'I can't tell you how much this day has meant to me,' he said.

She smiled. 'You've been an absolute dear, and I've enjoyed it too.'

The proprietor almost rushed to greet two people entering the taverna. The woman went into the back room to wash her hands and the man stood by the old fig tree shading one of the tables, cupping a ripe fig in his hand. He plucked it from the tree and peeled back the skin. He glanced up and saw the man with the girl's hand in his and the shared smile. He sucked the fig dry and threw down the skin, then followed the Greek woman into the kitchen. When he came out, the couple had gone.

Samantha had to back the car to get it out of the small space left by the Bugatti that almost blocked the path, and she eyed it with loathing. It was a symbol of everything the man represented. He must have the best, in cars and land and women, and he didn't care in whose way he thrust his possessions.

'All right?' asked Ben, anxiously.

'Fine,' she said. 'But I have to concentrate on the road. It will be busy with evening traffic once we reach the main road, so if I'm a bit silent, you'll know why.'

He settled down and left her to her thoughts and wondered why she drove so fast when they had already eaten. There was no hurry to get back. Few cars were going in the direction of the village, and a steady stream of traffic converged on the turning to one of the bigger tourist towns. Silhouettes of small shrines and waving tree tops were darkening as late dusk powdered the warm island.

The lights of the village glinted across the bridge and the dust from the road made the change from tarmac and gravel evident. The car springs creaked and Samantha slowed to a more cautious speed.

'Isn't that the place where the turtles swim?' said Ben. 'I haven't seen them yet and Brendan was telling me about them.'

'I doubt if we can see them now, and I've no idea if they come out at night. We should have brought some biscuits.'

'Can we stop for a minute and you can tell me where you saw them. I can come early tomorrow and feed them if I wake up in time,' said Ben.

'You might see something,' said Samantha, 'but I hardly think it's worth it. There's very little light until the moon comes up.'

As if to contradict her, the bright three-quarters moon burst from behind a cloud, throwing deep shadows from the silver-topped trees.

'She's on your side,' said Samantha, and

116

laughed as she climbed from the car. They walked along to the bridge, enjoying the warm scent of broom and herbs and the silence of the empty road.

'It amazes me how suddenly the cicadas switch off,' said Ben. 'Did you notice back there in the taverna how they were suddenly silent at a certain point of darkness?'

'No,' she said. Any sudden silence for her had come when the man with the Bugatti had arrived with his lovely companion. Any silence then had been because her heart stopped beating until it beat faster in fury and jealousy when she was blocked in by the wonderful car. She wondered where they were and if the moon shone softly on the woman's black hair and made a gleam of love appear in the man's proud eyes. 'What did you say?'

'I thought I saw a turtle over there.' Ben dropped a twig into the water and the ripples carried to the shore. 'No, they're not here,' he said, but made no move back to the car. 'Dreaming?' he asked.

'No, just enjoying the cooler air,' lied Samantha. 'I think that even a sun-worshipper can have too much of the heat in Corfu. I've bought everything I need there and I shall stay by the sea tomorrow.'

Ben came closer and put an arm across her shoulder. It was a warm, friendly feeling and she didn't move away. They watched the moon on the stream and listened to late rustlings as tiny creatures went about their nocturnal wanderings. The moon was brighter than she had known it since coming to Corfu. It grew bigger each night and would become full in a few nights' time. If only I could love a man like Ben, she thought. He's good and kind and very considerate, the complete opposite to the brash, extrovert rally drivers that her father encouraged to come to the house. She shivered slightly as she recalled the memories that had become blurred under Greek blue skies. With Ben at her side, she now knew that all men were not beasts, that there were gentle beings ready with love and devotion, and she didn't turn away when he kissed her gently on the cheek. Dear Ben... Why not let him think that she was heart-whole? It did no harm, and the time would come when she would have to settle for someone like him, even if it was second best.

From the main road came the sweep of powerful headlights as a fast car came through the dust cloud. Samantha leaned back against the bridge with Ben's arm still round her shoulders. They watched the car come closer and Samantha gulped hard to stop herself from gasping. The Bugatti swept up to the potholed bridge and slowed as they had done. The headlights picked out moths flying into the beams and the driver held the steering wheel in firm brown hands. His glance swept over the couple by the bridge and he sounded the musical klaxon horn as if in anger.

He had gone and the moon fled behind a wisp of cloud. 'Let's get back. Carla will think we're lost,' she said. She drove back and parked the car, refusing Ben's offer of a visit to Maik's.

'I'm very tired,' she said. 'I'll see if Carla is OK and get to bed. Thanks for dinner, Ben. And I did enjoy Corfu.' She slipped away from his restraining hand, knowing that he wanted to kiss her, and ran up the outside stairway to her room.

The light was on in the next room and she tapped on the door. 'Where have you been?' said Carla. She lay on her bed, fully dressed and looking far less pink than she had been at breakfast. 'We thought you'd be back for dinner.'

'I doubt if you missed us,' said Samantha. 'Had a good day?' Carla nodded. 'I enjoyed Corfu, but it was very hot. I bought your films and took some good shots of shrines. We saw the coins like the one I have, and Ben insisted on giving me dinner at a very nice taverna half way up a mountain.'

'You don't *have* to tell me all the details.' Carla was laughing. 'I'm not your chaperone. We fed the turtles and did nothing and it was great. The taverna was nearly empty all day as most of the guests went on a Stavros Special trip to Benitsis for a knees-up.'

'No excitement at all?'

'Oh, yes – something that will interest you, I hope. Eva came to us in a tizz. She had heard from Mr Gaia that he is planning a barbecue and party the day after tomorrow, and he wants her to make her special moussaka and some cream cakes.'

'How does that concern us? We aren't likely to be invited,' said Samantha coldly.

'Eva has a van which she uses to fetch supplies from Corfu and the ferry, but it's in the garage for repairs. She has to have someone to take the goodies up to his house on the day of the party and she wondered if we'd help. Stavros has a party booked for Corfu town and a visit to a monastery, so he can't do it. And the other cars are all hired out.'

'So is ours! We might want it for

something. We haven't been to Kassiopi yet,' said Samantha indignantly. 'What's to stop her asking the other people who hired Stavros' cars?'

'You are a good driver and it *is* over a few hairpin bends. I think she wants her moussaka to arrive in one piece.'

'I can't think that Rhexenor Gaia would approve of me having anything to do with it.'

'That's where you are mistaken. He now knows that you are the daughter of John Beauchamp, whom he met a few times some years ago.' Carla grinned. 'I expect the poor man thinks he's made one almighty faux pas and wants to do the polite thing.'

'I can't imagine it, and if he does, then I shall feel even more anti-Mr Gaia. I'd rather be asked for myself than for any fame that's rubbed off on me from my father! I think you're mistaken, Carla. We shall be asked to deliver the food and then be expected to leave, like obedient little girls.'

'Eva said we were invited to the party. She

wants us to take her and the food up early, then come back for some more cakes from the freezer and stay for the barbecue.'

'Gilt-edged invitations, I suppose?' said Samantha sarcastically.

'Don't be like that. It should be fun. I'm dying to see his house, and Eva said that it's the first time he has opened the place to visitors since his wife died. Something must have woken him up to make him change.'

'I know what it is – or who it is,' said Samantha.

'Oh, who is it? Eva was very surprised when I told her he did the table dance. She couldn't think how it happened.'

'He's in love with a very beautiful Greek woman,' said Samantha, trying to sound as if she was giving a series of rather boring facts. 'I saw them together in Corfu and again on the road to Afionis. He must have driven her in the Bugatti and left her there. He came back about the same time that we did.'

'But he came back before you. There was

no mistaking that engine.'

'They had a drink at the taverna where we ate. We left first, but he caught us up on the way back.' Carla eyed her with amused suspicion. 'Ben wanted to see the turtles, so we stopped for a few minutes by the bridge,' said Samantha.

'And how many did you see, at dead of night?'

'It wasn't like that,' said Samantha tersely. 'Ben isn't my type and he only wanted to see the turtles.'

'I believe you,' said Carla, 'but thousands wouldn't. Are you coming down to Maik's?'

'No, I told Ben I was going to bed.'

'Oh, come on! I waited for you. Brendan has gone to put new film in his camera and to write a couple of cards, and I said we'd meet him later when you got back.'

'I don't feel like it. I'm still hot.'

'Have a shower and slip into that spectacular kaftan thing you bought in Corfu. We could go for a walk along the shore and get some air if you like.'

'Oh, very well.'

Samantha went to her own room and undressed. She looked along the shore but saw nothing moving but the gentle rise and fall of the sea under an indigo sky. Small clouds hid the moon and teased the earth with brief glimpses of her brightness. Samantha was cooler and less mentally ruffled when she tapped again on the other door.

'You look like a Greek lady! With that tan and your dark hair, you are more Greek than the Greeks,' Carla exclaimed.

The long line of the soft cotton robe made Samantha seem taller and the full skirt swept behind her as she walked down the stairs. Deep turquoise and rose splashed with ochre and pale violet made an impact as arresting as the colours on an artist's palette, and her hair was curling damply at the ends after the shower.

Samantha experienced a moment of panic as she went into the café, but the nimbus of deep auburn hair was not there and she sighed – with a mixture of relief and disappointment. I'm being ridiculous, she told herself. I should avoid every opportunity of seeing him, not half-hope that he will appear wherever I go.

Her cheeks warmed as she wondered what impression he had formed when he saw her with Ben Mathers, first holding hands across the café table and then standing close together in the moonlight by the romantic old bridge. Had he seen the protective arm across her shoulders? It's no concern of his, and what does it matter? she told herself. He thinks nothing of me as a woman, and now I have the embarrassment of having to meet him and make polite conversation because he remembers my father. She wrinkled her brow. Where had they met? Cars must be the common interest. Could the Bugatti really be the same one that she had seen when she was still a schoolgirl?

'Not many here tonight.' Carla looked around the café, nodded to Hebe and sat at a corner table where they could watch the people coming in. Samantha sat where she could see and not be seen too clearly, belatedly self-conscious of the rather extreme dress she was wearing.

Brendan paused in the doorway and smiled when he saw Carla.

'I can see that your day was a success,' said Samantha dryly. 'He looks as if he's the cat with the cream.'

'You be quiet, Sam. Don't tell him I own Brooklyn Bridge. I want to be loved for me alone.'

'I think you're serious,' said Samantha.

'Hi there! We saved a few dozen seats for you,' said Carla.

'Just as well. The crowd from the hotel are coming. We're being invaded by the escapees from the concrete monstrosity over the headland. Some rotter must have told them that we have more fun here than they do.'

In a few minutes every table was full and Maik was smiling. He grinned as he put on modern pop music, reading his customers preferences correctly and shrugging his shoulders when Brendan asked for Greek music. 'I suppose they are bringing in the money tonight,' said Brendan, 'but I'm not dancing to that.'

A man in a tight tee-shirt and well-patched jeans asked Samantha to dance, but she shook her head. It wasn't the same atmosphere as the previous night and she knew that she had no desire to dance with an unattractive stranger.

Ben came in and looked surprised and rather annoyed. 'I thought you weren't coming,' he said. 'I'd have come earlier.'

'I had to drag her along,' said Carla. 'She said she was tired, but a shower and change soon put that right, and here she is as good as new.'

'Better. You look very good, Samantha.'

She smiled and wished that he didn't have that look in his eyes. I shall hate leaving here, she thought, but you could ruin this place for me if you try to monopolise my company. 'I shan't stay long,' she said.

'I was talking to Mr Gaia,' Ben said. 'He is very interesting when you get to know him. We had a drink at Eva's bar and he showed me some old coins he carried with him for luck. One was just like the turtle coin you showed me, Samantha.'

'I hope you didn't tell him about it.'

'Of course I did. He was fascinated. I was surprised at the interest he showed. After all, he had several there that were of greater value than yours – even older – but he said he'd like to see the one you have.'

'I haven't brought it with me,' said Samantha.

'That doesn't matter. He said he could see it when you come to his party. I didn't know you had been invited.'

'We're the milk run, delivering the food,' said Samantha. 'That hardly makes us invited.'

'Oh, he said he had told Eva to invite you and Carla.'

'I don't take invitations at second-hand,

and he had no need to do so just because he knew my father.'

'Ah, that would explain it. He has to invite you, to be the polite Greek host to the daughter of an old friend. The Greeks take hospitality very seriously.' Ben looked relieved.

Samantha tried to smile. 'I think he is only now coming out of mourning for his wife and has another lady-love.'

'I'm relieved to hear it. He was much too interested in you for my peace of mind, Samantha. I suppose he was recalling the time when he knew your father. They must be about the same age,' he added, with an air of satisfaction.

'He isn't old,' said Samantha, 'that is, if he was a contemporary of my father, he would still be young. My parents married in their teens, and I'd hardly think that Mr Gaia was a father figure.'

'No, Eva said that his wife was pregnant when she died, so he hasn't the son he longed for.'

So he too, wanted a son, passionately, thought Samantha. Another reason for avoiding marriage with a man like that. He'd have a fixation like my father about having a son and heir to carry on the same interests, to live the same life again. She blushed. Why had she thought of marriage? She tried to tell herself that she was thinking of any male chauvinist, but her glance went to the door and she wondered if he would come in, stare round the room with that arrogant head held high and wait for service.

It was midnight and her eyes were heavy. The long hot day was over and the night air was still warm enough for both girls to walk from the café without jackets. The two men had gone, and Carla stood on the tiny landing by the apartment, gazing at the sea.

'Let's walk,' suggested Samantha. 'It was smoky in there and the noise of the disco was terrible. I can't think how people can come to a lovely place like this and opt for that kind of music when there is such good authentic local music.'

'I'm for bed. I need sleep,' moaned Carla. 'Don't be long and take care.' She unlocked the door and eased herself inside. 'My sunburn is itching. I'm going to smother myself in cream and lie on the top of the bedclothes in the raw.'

'Well, better lock the door! I've got my key.'

Samantha walked along by the silent shops, thinking that she would go as far as Eva's taverna, where a few lights were still burning. The outer café was empty and she could see three people sitting inside at one of the tables, a bottle of wine before them. Softly, Samantha slid by the taverna, hoping that she was unobserved. The moon came out with sudden brilliance, turning the dark sea to silver and the swinging bottles on the awning roof into jewels of beauty instead of the dusty-coloured glass they were by day. She sat on the wall and watched a light far out to sea. Across the water came the cry of a fisherman as he called to another boatman to lift the nets. It was peaceful, warm and good, and she should have been content. But she couldn't forget that one of the figures drinking wine with Eva and Iannis was Rhexenor Gaia.

The moon seemed to hypnotise her as she gazed into the distance, and she heard nothing but the soft lapping of water and the crumbling shingle as it dried. Then a flurry of red fur bounded from the taverna and a voice called, 'Ariel?' Samantha tried to stand, in an effort to escape before the man saw her. Stupid! she thought. Of course he'd take his dog out last thing at night. Ariel sensed her nearness and barked. He ran down and greeted her with joy, trying to convince her that she was his one true friend.

'Ariel!' The dark shadow emerged from the wall and became a man. Rhexenor Gaia seemed even bigger and more dominant with the moon making ripples of light in his thick bright hair. His face seemed almost gaunt where the shadows etched depth to his eyes and the firm chin was jutting with annoyance and curiosity. 'Come here. Bad dog.'

Samantha rose to her feet unsteadily, her hand on the collar of the dog.

'Oh, it's you,' said a deep voice. 'Do you spend your time trying to alienate the affections of my dog, Miss Beauchamp?' She couldn't make out whether he was angry or merely being sarcastic. The firm lips curved into a smile and she saw the amused glitter of his eyes.

'I was walking before going to bed,' she said with dignity. 'I thought I had the beach to myself.' She turned away. 'Goodnight, Mr Gaia.'

The dog followed her and rubbed against her, whining softly. 'He doesn't want you to go,' said Rhexenor Gaia.

'Go on, back to your master,' said Samantha, but Ariel still followed her. 'You'll have to put him on a lead,' she said.

'That seems a pity.' The voice was only

faintly mocking. 'Come with us as far as the bridge and he can run free.' He took a step away from her. 'Come,' he said, and she had no power to refuse.

She walked slowly, as if her feet refused to obey her. The dog ran before them, now that the stupid humans had taken his meaning and were walking together. The long, graceful kaftan swayed as she walked over the rough ground, her high-heeled sandals slipping on the smoother pebbles.

'You didn't come dressed for a walk,' he said.

'I had no intention of doing so. I think I'll go back,' she said.

'We're almost there. Don't you want to pay homage to the turtles of Corfu?' The mockery was back in the deep warm voice.

'Do they expect homage every time you pass them?'

'I think so.' He glanced at her profile and saw the moonlight glowing on the beautiful darkness that was her hair. 'Perhaps – who knows? – the old gods sacrificed beautiful maidens to the turtles, as they did to Athena to send fair winds.'

'I hope the custom has died,' said Samantha.

They reached the bridge. 'I think that offerings are still made to them.'

'I've seen children feeding them,' said Samantha, trying to keep her voice steady. He was so close to her that the warmth of his breath was on her cheek. He bent his head to look in the stream, and she saw the firm outline of the man – or was it the god Pan with curling hair and wicked eyes? She saw the veil of darkness from the shadowy girl so close to the man as her hair fell forwards, hiding her face.

'I wasn't thinking of bread,' he said, 'I hope that you were not sacrificing too much at the bridge tonight.'

Her cheeks burned. 'How dare you? I was showing a fellow guest where the turtles live.'

'That's good, to be helpful.' He was laughing at her and she was speechless. If she made excuses for Ben being with her, with his arm round her, she was admitting that there was something between them. Let him think what he liked, she thought. What concern was it of his, when he had a woman he loved? He walked back with her to the foot of the stairs. The moon was playing tricks behind light cloud again and she couldn't read his eyes. He held out a hand and took one of hers. 'I was sorry to hear about your father. I met him and liked him,' he said simply. 'Tell me, Miss Beauchamp, is he very badly crippled?'

'Oh no.' Her dark eyes looked at him, directly for the first time. 'It took time and care and surgery, but he is walking almost normally and is quite independent now.'

'So you can now take a holiday after caring for him for so long?'

'How did you know I looked after him?'

'Your new friend told Eva quite a lot about you. It is good to see you took your duties seriously.'

'And now, I can please myself,' she said,

lightly. 'I can do as I wish and make a career for myself.'

'Women should have homes and children,' he said.

'It doesn't follow that a woman wants to be married,' she said defiantly. 'A woman these days doesn't need a man to provide a home, so there is no need to marry unless she wishes it.'

'Does that mean you believe in free love?'

'No of course not. It means that a woman need never marry just for a home. It leaves her free to find the man she really wants, and if she is wise she makes an interesting career while she is single.'

'And you will love.' He glanced at the stubborn set of her chin. 'You will learn what love can do to you and you will be helpless.'

'No!' It sounded too vehement even to her. 'I can do without men.'

'You have been hurt, but I think you have not loved,' he said calmly.

'And I suppose you know all about love?'

She regretted the words, knowing he had suffered a great loss.

'I married and lost her.' He seemed to be talking to himself. 'We married young because our parents wished it, and she was good and beautiful. I was grief-stricken when she died because I lost a true friend, but only now have I seen what love can do to a man.' His eyes were deep and sombre.

'And she is very beautiful. I saw her today and she will make you very happy.' The words were forced out of her. I can never have you, so I must be generous in my praise, she thought.

'You saw Cassiami? Of course, you were on the mountains with your fellow-guest again.' He seemed to think that her being with Ben Mathers was a joke. 'You saw us come to the taverna, before I took her to Aflonis.' He smiled. 'I shall look forward to you both meeting at my party. You are coming and bringing that nice pink American.' Samantha smiled. 'It is kind of you to help Eva, but I'm beginning to know that you are a very kind person.' He raised her hand to his lips. 'I salute you,' he said, and the light kiss was warm and sent tremors of exquisite pain into her heart.

She tried to draw away but his lips were on her wrist and in the tender hollow of her elbow. He took her into his arms with a sweeping movement that gathered her to his heart, and his kiss brought her mouth into submission. Then he released her.

'It was the voice of the turtle, it whispered of love,' he said. 'Goodnight, Samantha, come soon to my home in the mountain.' He waved and laughed like an old-time cavalier and swung away, racing his dog until his shadow was no more on the empty quay.

Samantha put a trembling hand to her face and the tears fell on the beautiful colours of her dress, in shame that he thought her a mixture of slave to her father, hard career woman and yet a woman who took and gave kisses lightly.

5

'The house should tell us something about him,' said Carla. 'I can't wait to see where that beautiful man lives. Eva said that he never, but never, lets outsiders into his domain – and she should know. She's known him all her life, or all of his life, rather. She talks of taking him for walks when he was little.'

'I can't imagine him ever being a child,' said Samantha. 'He was born with that arrogant thrust to his chin.' She carefully avoided a patch of grass near the edge of the road, thinking that it might hide a ditch. The sun was high and the cicadas were busily trying to drown every other sound on the mountain. A hawk hovered lazily on a thermal of warm air and seemed in no hurry to swoop on to his prey. 'We have another journey like this one later, so we'd better get there as quickly as we can and have our picnic lunch on the way down.'

'I'd rather stick around up there.'

'No, it wouldn't do,' said Samantha. 'We shall have plenty of time tonight to see the place officially. I have no intention of laying myself open to any more of his sarcasm, or worse.' Her mind still refused to focus on the events of the night, when Rhexenor Gaia had kissed her as if she gave kisses readily to anyone who demanded them. Since then, she hadn't seen him. In the morning, his car had gone and the catamaran went out, piloted by Spiro as if he was ferrying it round to the other side of the mountain. Her confidence grew as the day went on, knowing that he wasn't likely to appear, but there was an undercurrent of disappointment, as though she missed him in spite of her tension when he was there. And now she felt light-hearted, and the thought of meeting him held no terrors. 'I expect, he's busy in Corfu town or wherever he has offices,' she said, 'but I shall still wait until tonight to see the place properly.'

They rounded the next bend and the house was revealed. It was old and rambling, with a lovely tiled roof and sloping gables. The driveway led round a central flower bed, which was a riot of scarlet geraniums and evergreen bushes. The scent of the last of the broom blossom hung heavily, and Samantha thought she could smell jasmine.

Eva bustled out of the wide doorway to take some of the trays of food and a cool box packed with more perishable items. She hurried into the kitchens with the huge moussaka, and Carla and Samantha brought in the rest.

'You are very kind,' said Eva. 'It will all be well tonight.' She looked anxious. 'You *will* come with the other cakes?' Samantha smiled and nodded. 'Kyria Cassiami is looking after the tables, and the men are building the pit for the fire over there by the view from that side. It will be as it was, but no Kyria Gaia.'

'Who is the Kyria Cassiami?' asked Carla.

'She is the sister of Rhexenor's wife, and she will be the second wife, I think, if she has her way.'

'And Mr Gaia?' Carla paused, and Eva shrugged. 'Does he say that he will marry the lovely Cassiami?'

'I know nothing. I think today of food only. I can say nothing.'

'I don't think she approves of Cassiami,' said Carla, as the car edged along a narrow part of the road.

'She's probably jealous of anyone who looks at her beloved Rhexenor,' said Samantha. 'She's known him for so long that she resents anyone, however suitable.'

'Perhaps she fancies him for herself?' They laughed at the thought of the ungainly Eva having hopes of marrying a man who could choose from any number of beautiful women.

'Let's stop here,' said Carla. They un-packed the pitta bread stuffed with salad, and the feta cheese and fruit. Iannis had included a half bottle of wine and some water, and Samantha diluted the wine until it was just a refreshing drink. The view from the far side of the track was superb and they scrambled down to a terrace where ancient olive trees bent under their weight of rich black fruit.

'England seems so far away,' said Samantha dreamily. 'I could stay here for ever.'

'Marry a Corfiot and live here,' said Carla. 'I prefer to come for holidays.'

'With a husband and children?'

'Something like that.' Carla blushed and broke a dry twig that had fallen on her lap, and once again, Samantha felt a twinge of envy for the girl who would marry the man she loved. She looked down at the winding road they must take to get back to the village. She saw the twisting paths through grey-green olive groves with goats tethered in the shade and sheep being driven by women in black with small children. It was leisured and dignified with the counterpoint of hardness making the sunlit days even more beautiful.

They drove down slowly when they had finished eating, and stopped again to admire the view of the sea. 'It all looks so pure and clean and innocent,' said Samantha, and shivered. 'It *does* look safe,' she said, but an inner doubt made her turn away as if there was a threat hidden beneath the calm blue face of the ocean. Would life always be like that for her? Would it show her the beautiful side and then destroy any trust she had built up?

'I shall remember this place for as long as I live,' she said. 'When I go back, I think I can put events into perspective. I could see nothing clearly at home.'

'Nothing seems as bad from a distance, and nothing quite as good. I know what I want now, and I shall fight to get it,' said Carla.

'Brendan?'

'Yes. I shall do as I think fit and ask

nobody for permission,' said Carla. 'My family had a guy all lined up for me, so I quit. I have no intention of going back until I have Brendan with me.'

'Does he know this?'

'Not yet, but he's getting the message,' said Carla.

The village was quiet in the afternoon heat and the girls lay on their beds for an hour until the worst of the mid-day heat was gone. Samantha lay in a half-sleep, tired after the drive to the house on Afionis and half-dreading the evening to come. There would be crowds of guests, and having made his one gesture towards remembering her father, Rhexenor Gaia might not even see her during the evening, especially as most of his party would be out of doors in semi-darkness. His duties as host, with the help of the beautiful woman who had gone to Afionis to be near him, would take all his time and he could make sure he didn't meet anyone he wanted to avoid.

Carla was very excited and came and sat on Samantha's bed long before it was time to change and start again for the villa.

'We can't take the cakes and baklava from the fridge yet or they'll be warm by the time they get eaten. From the appearance of the kitchen at Afionis, there won't be room for any more in the fridges, so we ought to wait a while,' said Samantha.

'I can't think how you can lie there when there is so much to see. I want to have a good look around the house before the party. I love poking about in other people's homes,' said Carla complacently. 'I might get some ideas for my own when I have one.'

'It's much too early. Is Brendan coming? What time are we picking him up, if he needs a lift?'

'You aren't going to believe this, but we are the only ones invited. Eva actually produced our formal invitations and sent Iannis along with them.'

'We're going alone?' Samantha could hardly believe it. 'I suppose he had to invite us as we were helping Eva. What do we do now? Wait at table and hand round canapés?'

'I intend to enjoy myself, whatever motives the man might have. I think he really wanted just you, but had to invite me to go with you. I'm not proud. I don't mind if I have to go in the back door if I'm allowed the run of that heavenly house for half an hour. I shall take some film and flashes with me, and it will be the highlight of my holiday. It isn't every one who has an invitation from one of the most important men on the island. If I can get some really Greek pictures, I shall be happy.'

'I want to wander in the olive groves and imagine what it was like in ancient times.'

'When Odysseus sailed in and was shipwrecked?' Carla smiled. 'Eva called you Nausicaa. Be around when *The Flying Turtle* is thrown up on the rocks... Odysseus might need you.'

'He has his princess at the villa,' said Samantha. She stood by the window and looked across the sea. There was hardly a ripple and the sun shone as if it were glued to the heavens and could never change the sky. 'I can't imagine a rough sea here, certainly not bad enough to wreck a boat. The catamaran looks strong and it has engines, unlike the old sailboats. Some of them had oarsmen, I believe, but nothing as fast as engine power. I'd love to sail in *The Flying Turtle*,' she said wistfully.

'Perhaps Mr Gaia will stay in the villa with his lady love and Stavros will hire it to us for an afternoon. Let's ask him, Sam. We could all go, the four of us.' Carla glowed with enthusiasm. 'I'll ask. I don't mind making the arrangements and it would be fun. Romantic, too.'

'I doubt if it's for hire,' said Samantha.

She brushed her hair and opened her wardrobe. The kaftan hung like a brightly-winged butterfly with wings folded. Her heart beat faster as she touched it. The last time she had worn it, heaven had shown her what joy and pain there could be in a hard embrace, in the delicate tracery of kisses on her bare arm and in the delirium of a kiss. She pushed it to one side and chose the coffee and cream dress with the low neck-line as the evening would be warm. She shook out the fold of a silky shawl she had bought in the town. The soft fringe ran though her fingers and she traced the edge of the intricate embroidery in the corner. The rich colours of the silk threads made a picture of exotic birds and flowers, and the background was the same colour as her cream dress.

'Mosquitoes might be bad,' she said, to justify taking the pretty and flattering cover.

'I'll take a jacket – I've got a thin cotton one,' said Carla. 'I need to have my hands free for the camera.' She laughed. 'You can swan about looking glamorous and make every Greek man's heart beat faster, but I want pictures.'

'Don't be silly,' said Samantha. 'Nobody will notice me among so many. I expect there'll be a lot of very smart women there.'

But she took care to make sure that her lipstick was right and her eyes were shadowed with a touch of smudgy darkness.

The tray of food and the two cool containers were stowed in the boot, and a rather disconsolate Brendan waved them off, saying that he might as well go with Ben to the evening concert at the hotel across the headland. 'Don't forget to feed the turtles,' called Carla maliciously.

'No fun without you,' he said, and she smiled as she settled into the car for the drive up the mountain.

The evening light was still bright enough to see clearly without car lights when they came to the villa. Already, several cars were parked in the driveway and a space for more had been cleared beneath some trees.

Samantha drove up to the front door to deliver the food and was met by a beaming Eva, dressed in a vast tent of shocking pink cotton. She took some of the containers and the girls followed with the others.

'Come,' she said. 'I show you the house.'

'But are you sure he won't mind?' asked Samantha, afraid to intrude on the closely guarded privacy of the man who had been rude to her because she had dared to sit in his car uninvited.

'He is busy,' chuckled Eva. 'He will not know, and if he does he will not be angry. Today he is happy. He is back in the world with his friends and we all rejoice. He cannot be angry today.'

'I hope you're right,' said Samantha with feeling.

They walked through the lower rooms, revelling in the coolness inside the thick walls and the deep shade in the alcoves under the overhanging balconies of the upper rooms. Wide windows were open to the air, and the scent of orange blossom and jasmine came through the rooms, gently perfuming the whole house. Pictures of Greek islands hung in the main hall, but in a study lined with books there were good modern paintings by European artists. All were chosen to fit in perfectly with the decor, and the effect was one of flamboyance and colour.

'Is it as it was when his wife was alive?' asked Carla.

'The other rooms are the same, but the study is where he sits and plays music. He has a room for guns for the chase in winter and another for the games.' Eva flung open door after door, and the pattern of Rhexenor Gaia's life emerged.

Samantha could feel the attraction and peace of the villa. It was perfect for work and play and for living. Her heart beat faster when they went up to the next floor and were shown two guest rooms. He slept here, she thought, but was rather glad that Eva didn't include an inspection of his private suite in the tour. Several doors were shut fast and she could only imagine what was behind them. Was he busy in one of the rooms with the lovely Greek woman he had brought from the ferry?

Carla had no inhibitions. 'Where is the

Greek lady he brought here? I take it she's staying for the party?'

Eva pursed her lips. 'She is very busy, that one. She tries to do everything when Rhexenor can see her. She works if he is here, to show him how well she would be as mistress of the villa. She is here because she is his sister-in-law, but she would like to be more.'

'He must have invited her,' said Carla bluntly.

'Yes, it is so. She suggested this party months ago, but it was only this week that he suddenly decided to give it any thought. He wrote to her inviting her, and she came early to make sure all was ready, as she said.' They regained the hall as the light softened into sunset. 'I must go to the kitchens. There is wine on the long tables out there and, later, food. Go and see the garden and look at the sunset. Is good?'

'I have to take a shot of that. Get those colours, Sam!'

'I'll wander down there while it's light

enough to see,' said Samantha. 'Those olive trees must be centuries old.'

She was glad she had worn a dress shorter than the kaftan as she picked her way over gnarled roots and came to an opening between the trees. The sun hovered over a veil of pastel colour, shaking out a shawl over the sea. The pathway across the water was silver-gilt and the heads of the fishermen in the tiny caique were bronze figurines on a plaque of blue steel. A breath of air stirred the dry leaves, and she glanced up at the grey-green bark of the olives. Tall cyprus trees arrowed the hillside, and Samantha looked down with a full heart.

'I've never seen anything as beautiful,' she said. She turned, thinking to find Carla behind her.

'I'm flattered, and I think what I see is beautiful, too.' The voice was deep and the sombre eyes were not looking at the view.

Samantha tossed the dark hair from her glowing face with a hand that was startlingly brown against the pale shawl. She bent down to touch the dog, who had come running towards them, and Rhexenor Gaia gazed at the thick dark hair hanging low over the dog's neck and the sweet line of her cleavage under the simple lace bodice. She looked up and surprised an expression of sad tenderness in his eyes. Her eyelids fluttered to hide her confusion and he bent to tap the dog gently on the muzzle.

'He's very good,' said Samantha.

Rhexenor Gaia smiled slowly. 'You have a saying in England: "Love my dog and you will love me."'

She laughed, glad the tension was broken. 'Not quite,' she said. 'It's love me, love my dog.'

'It is the same. He is mine and we both need love.'

'Who doesn't?' she said lightly. 'Why are you having a party just now, Mr Gaia?'

'Eva has been bullying me for months. Come and see what we are doing. The pit for the barbecue is over there, but we will walk this side first so that you can see my land.'

Her heavy cotton skirt clung to her legs as they walked slowly through the grove. She glanced at his pale green silk shirt and tight black linen trousers.

He sighed. 'It is like so many things. I let time pass and do nothing because I do not know if I want people in my house, or even if people want to come.' He shrugged. 'I found there were many people who still wanted to be invited to Afionis.'

'How could you doubt it? You know so many people in Corfu and you must have many friends. Who would refuse an invitation to such a wonderful place?'

'I have many acquaintances, few friends.' His pure profile was sad as he stared out over the last rosy glow in the sky and Samantha felt an upsurge of compassion for him. He still loves her and misses her, she thought, and a tiny sliver of ice seemed to enter her heart.

'Is that the barbecue?' she said.

They hurried towards another glow that was fast obliterating the glow in the sky. Below the clearing was a terrace framing yet another perfect picture-postcard view. Two men were feeding a trough-shaped pit with chips of wood, raking the glowing ashes to make a hot bed over which they laid steel grills. Piles of food waited on trestle tables, and pitta bread covered huge trays, awaiting the grilled meats. The first sizzle of souvlaki went on the grills, then the first hamburgers and the first lamb chops, and more wine was brought in huge pottery jugs to fill the ceramic goblets. A rising blur of voices in Greek and English grew as more guests arrived, and Samantha was increasingly conscious of the man who stood with her, silently watching as if this was not of his doing, these people who intruded on his privacy and disturbed the peace of sunset with their chatter.

'You must go to your guests,' she said.

'First I must show you something. Come!'

He led her back to the house. The hall was

deserted and the distant sounds from the party came faintly through the open windows. 'In here,' he said, and unlocked a door.

Samantha noticed that it was one of the doors that Eva had made no attempt to open when they were in the house, and she realised that she was about to enter a room which Rhexenor Gaia kept private, away from casual observers.

Samantha looked up at the spartan elegance of the cool, uncluttered room. The floors were tiled in soft colours, with pictures of dolphins and fish, goddesses and turtles, and Poseidon with tumbling hair and fierce trident. The walls were richly decorated, and through an archway was an inner courtyard where trees grew by a rushing cascade of water.

She smiled, glad that she had bought the simplified edition of Homer's *Odyssey* when she was in Corfu and had read much of it when she was resting. '"Brazen were the walls, silver were the lintels ... and the garden with twin fountains, its apple trees and fig trees ... pears and pomegranates..." Or words to that effect,' she said.

He smiled his pleasure. 'The palace of Alcinous. You know it.' The light in his eyes was the flicker of rapport of two souls meeting. 'You read Homer.' It was a statement, a discovery. He laughed lightly, sweeping a mocking bow. 'Then it is I who should be your guest. Will you take pity on a weary traveller, a latter-day Odysseus, Nausicaa of the House of Alcinous?'

She blushed. 'But you aren't shipwrecked on the shores of Kerkira.' Her eyelashes lay as dusky moths on her smooth cheeks.

'It was Phaeicia when Odysseus came,' he said. 'He was wrecked because of the anger of the gods.'

She glanced up and then away again, unable to face the sombre eyes. 'And it was ancient history, myths handed down and gathering at every telling,' she said.

'There are other shipwrecks that cast lonely men at the feet of lovely women, leaving them bruised and faint,' he said quietly. His hand was on her shoulder, his face close to hers and she felt the brush of his hair on her cheek. 'There comes a time after the storm when the traveller needs comfort, warm arms and a warm heart to bring him strength again, and peace.'

'And you have it again.' She tried to keep the tremor from her voice, and walked back into the hall away from the dangerous magic of that inner room. 'You have found her and she will make this a home again.' She had to keep a picture in her mind of the woman looking up at him, her face ready to receive his kiss of greeting.

'I have yet to meet your friend, but I have seen her and she is beautiful. She will bring everything you need to this place,' she said slowly, picking her words so that she would sound fair and objective and would give no hint of the turmoil of emotions that tore at her heart.

At the door, he took her firmly and raised her face so that she had to look up at him.

She stiffened, knowing that if he kissed her again as he had kissed her after the walk to the bridge, she would crumble, mentally and physically and he would have her completely in his power. He gazed down at her for a full minute, then gently put her from him.

'Your other guests...' she said weakly.

'My other guests, yes, I must go to them and see that they are fed.' There was veiled contempt in his voice, as if he were going to feed hounds or a sty of swine. He took her hand and kissed it, softly. 'And I must never desecrate the hospitality of the Princess Nausicaa. I must not make love to any women in her palace until I take a bride.' He laughed as if enjoying a secret joke. 'But you shall meet many interesting people, including Cassiami if you wish. I will take you now, and we must dance again. I have not shown you my turtle coins, but that must wait. Tomorrow, you will sail with me on my *Flying Turtle* we will compare old coins as friends, and you will tell me about your father, Samantha.'

The change from the serious, almost tragic, man to this vital, exuberant and charming creature was baffling. It was as if he switched off a dim light and lit a fire behind his eyes – a fire of determined humour that somehow lacked the sincerity of the man she had glimpsed in the inner courtyard.

A trio of players strummed softly and lights from the valley and the passing boats on the Aegean sea sparkled like fire-flies. Hot ashes glowed dull red as the steaks and souvlaki sizzled in olive oil, herbs and lemon juice and were received ecstatically by the hungry guests. Carla waved a lamb chop, and patted the tree-root on which she sat, for Samantha to join her.

She looked back but Rhexenor had gone. Samantha went to the fire and chose her food, then brought it back to Carla. A boy tilted a large amphora to pour wine into her cup. She absorbed the sounds, the

164

opalescent glow of the dying day and the smells of olive bark and spiced meat cooking. She sipped cold wine and tried to join in light conversation, but her inner consciousness was full of one man – a man with a troubled face and proud, wounded eyes. *He has so much and, until tonight I thought he must be content,* she mused. She accepted a souvlaki, unwrapped it from its paper napkin, and absent-mindedly nibbled the hot cubed meat and peppers on the long skewer. *Was he happy? Who could be miserable in such a place!* She looked through the dancing shadows and saw him sitting high in the cleft of a tree stump, Ariel at his feet. He was laughing. *Of course he's happy,* she thought. *He has all this and Cassiami, too.*

Why could she not forget a voice saying, *There are other shipwrecks.* Why did his dark face come between her and the fire's glow? The music increased in tempo and the voices became louder and less inhibited. Wine flowed and most of the food was consumed. Samantha let the atmosphere wash away all dark thoughts. Men danced on the level terrace and Rhexenor watched but refused to join them, making the excuse that he had guests to entertain. Eva arrived from the kitchen bearing more moussaka, and proceeded to eat a generous helping of her own making. Young boys offered baskets of fruit, and one came with a shallow tray lined with fig leaves on which lay fresh green figs.

Samantha reached for an orange and saw that Carla had gone again to take yet more shots of the party. 'Why not try one of my figs?' said the voice that still lingered in her brain. She looked up, and he selected two firm specimens, offering one to her.

'Thank you Mr Gaia, but I've never eaten a fresh fig.'

'I think the daughter of an old acquaintance could call me Rhexenor, don't you?'

'I've still never eaten a fig, and I doubt if I'd enjoy it,' she said, smiling slightly.

'You can eat oranges at any time – even in England in the rain,' he said, and sat on the tree-stump where Carla had left her jacket.

'Are they ripe? All green fruit at home is sour. I've had dried figs at Christmas, but I can't say I like them very much. How do you tell if one is ripe?'

She felt his body by her side, close in the confined dip of the wood. She sensed his bold glance and knew that the wine had made him less inhibited – or was it the wildness of the woodland, the haunt of spirits and mischievous gods? He grinned, and his face was suddenly very young and wicked.

He dropped one fig into her lap. 'Do as I do,' he said. 'One tells if a fig is ripe by pressing it gently and exploring its inner being, as one finds out the heart of a woman.'

Samantha stared, fascinated. 'How do you eat it?'

He saw her puzzled expression. 'The fig is an ancient fruit, very sacred. It is said to represent woman. It is cool and has a close fitting skin of pale green, like the shirt you wear on the beach. It is smooth and firm, yet delicate.' He watched her reactions, smiling as she blushed. He carefully split the base of the fruit with a knife. 'The fig is the shape of a woman's inner being, her very womb.' He peeled back the fruit in four segments. 'We do not cut the fruit or tear it, we take it delicately, tenderly, so that it is still sweet and unbruised, and we savour it with love, so.'

He took the sweet pale gold flesh, exposing the lining, and put it to his mouth, and all the while he watched the girl with dark hair who seemed turned to stone. His eyes glinted in the dimness and she remembered a lizard which had stared at her unblinkingly from a rock, keeping her gaze until it fled. I'm trapped, she thought. It was almost a moment of panic. His leg was close to her thigh, the incline of their seat forcing him closer all the time. He peeled the segments of the second fruit back, revealing its inner sweetness, and she took the fruit and ate it as he had done, held by his power.

A childhood memory flashed into her mind. What was it? Laura, the girl who was spirited away by goblins and ate the fruit of forgetfulness. She could recall very little of the poem, but eating this fruit was sharing it as if she shared herself with him. It was a pagan sacrament.

'Delicious,' she said, and bent forward to take a paper napkin to wipe her lips, and to escape his gaze. He took her hand and kissed it, drinking the pale juice of the fig.

'You will not leave me alone for ever?'

'If you invite us, we'd love to come back,' she said, her rapid heartbeats threatening to choke her. 'There's Carla waving. We must go back. And thank you, Rhexenor.'

'I shall hold you to your promise to join me on the *Turtle*,' he said.

'Are we going on that gorgeous cat?' asked Carla, flopping to the ground with her camera.

'Tomorrow,' said Samantha. She smiled maliciously. 'At what time shall *we* come, Rhexenor?'

For a moment, he looked as if he would deny that he had invited anyone to see his *Flying Turtle*, then the fierce eyes smiled with reluctant humour.

'You win,' he said softly to Samantha. 'It will be a pleasure if you will both come at ten and we can sail for an hour or so before returning to the taverna for lunch.' He looked directly at Samantha and said, 'It isn't a very long voyage that we shall make. I had planned something more exciting, but you shall at least ride my turtle.'

A slender figure dressed in a frothy white blouse and long black skirt came towards them. 'Rhexenor, aren't you going to introduce me to your friends?' Cassiami put a tiny hand on his arm and looked up at him adoringly. 'I like to know any friends who come to Afionis,' she said.

6

'Eat up! Your friend said nothing about snacks on board. It's a long time before lunch.' Carla took more bread and smothered it with glutinous-looking preserve.

'He isn't my friend,' said Samantha, crumbling a piece of bread between her fingers. 'He asked us to go sailing out of politeness. He thinks he should make some kind of polite gesture to the daughter of a man he once knew.' She sounded patient, as if explaining the situation not only to Carla but to herself. Why else would he have been so pleasant the night before? She thought back to the time when Carla had interrupted him: I shall never know now if he intended to make love to me because he had drunk enough wine to let him forget his duties of a host. 'Where are the two men?'

'Brendan is sitting on the wall hoping to be given a lift in the cat. He's hopping mad that he hasn't been invited and, I hope, a little jealous. Do you think I could pretend that Rhexenor Gaia has a passion for me? No, I guess not. You're his type, not me.'

'I keep telling you that he is only polite because he knew Dad. Where's Ben? Is he sitting on the wall, too?'

'No. I meant to tell you that he asked for the car this morning. He said he'd bring it back by lunch-time. If we are to be out this morning it seemed a waste, so I thought you'd say yes.'

'Good idea,' said Samantha, but wondered if Carla's innocent expression was all it seemed. If Brendan went with them, there would be four on the boat unless a party came with Rhexenor. 'Perhaps Cassiami will come,' said Samantha.

'Oh, *no!* That would spoil everything,' said Carla. She blushed. 'I thought it might be cosy, just the four of us.'

'Thanks very much, but I like to do my own pairing,' said Samantha coldly. 'I can think of nothing cosy about Rhexenor Gaia.'

Eva hurried in. 'The boat is coming round the headland. Rhexenor rang earlier to ask you to take swimming things in case you like to swim from the boat. Stavros left the dinghy here and Rhexenor asked if one of the men could row you out in it, taking a few things I have for him.'

'Eureka!' said Carla. 'No trouble at all, Eva. I know just the guy – all I hope is that he can row!'

Carla went out to tell Brendan that he would be going on the boat and Samantha went to collect their bags of towels and bikinis from the apartment.

The boat became a larger speck and the twin hulls could be seen clearly. Eva gave Brendan the packages for the boat and stood watching, shading her eyes with one hand.

'It's hot,' said Carla. 'I shall take a hat.'

'It might be windy later,' said Eva. 'It

173

happens quickly here. Stavros said that the signs were there. It is bad to think it will not blow, that wind. It is not safe to think it will be calm all the time. Pouff – a storm comes from the hills out of nothing.'

One or two guests stopped by the beach to see the beautiful vessel tie up to the mooring. There were envious sighs from men who had hoped to be able to hire a sailing boat and had not been able to do so, and mere interest from people who preferred to sit at a café table sipping cool drinks while others sailed on the wet water.

Rhexenor waved and Samantha's heart lurched with longing. He was in brief swimming trunks of bright blue, his chest brown and slightly moist from the sea and his hair drying in the slight breeze.

'He's been swimming already,' said Carla.

Brendan took the oars and managed to row the unpredictable rubber boat in a fairly straight line to the catamaran, and Rhexenor bent to take the painter. He helped Carla on board and told Brendan to hand up the packages. Samantha waited in the stern until the boat was clear, then edged her way to the bow. With most of the load gone, the boat was light and bouncy. She put up a hand to a rail and dragged herself close to the hull. She put a foot on the edge of the rubber boat and pulled on the rail. The rubber boat slewed away and she dangled over the water. Two hands grasped hers and she was lifted bodily into the boat. For a breathless moment, she felt the beating of a man's heart as he held her close, then he laughed and put her on the deck. 'I didn't think you wanted to swim so soon,' said Rhexenor.

'Thank you,' she said. 'That dinghy has a mind of its own.'

Carla and Brendan were already in-specting the boat, and in spite of his earlier unwillingness to have strangers on board, Rhexenor seemed pleased with their frank enjoyment of the roomy craft. The cabin space was generous because of the width of the craft, and the furnishings were luxurious. A walnut drinks cabinet was bolted to the floor of the saloon, and the fragile glasses were secured behind firm leather straps that held everything still, however choppy the seas might be.

'It can get rough, and in force eight anything not secure is hurled about the deck,' Rhexenor explained.

'That must be fun,' said Samantha.

'Do you think so? Will you promise to come with me one day alone?' He handed her a drink and she lowered her eyelashes.

'If it was as rough as that, you'd need a crew,' she said demurely.

Carla came back from the deck.

'Drinks are ready, Carla,' said Samantha. It was becoming fun to be the one who did the teasing instead of being at the receiving end of the banter, rudeness or frank appraisal from a man who was attracted to her in passing, even when he was in love with another woman.

'I am sorry if I am keeping you all from your friend,' he said. His glance directed the words to Samantha.

'He's here with Brendan, but he has matters to see to in Corfu,' said Carla. 'He's a dedicated historian.'

'I thought that you were all together.' He moved away to look out at the sea, and only Samantha heard him. 'You seemed very attached to him and he looks on you with eyes of love.'

'He's sweet and courteous,' said Samantha. 'The kind of man a woman can trust and be safe with.'

Rhexenor drained his glass. 'How very British and how very dull,' he said calmly. 'It would grieve me if any woman I brought here thought she was safe.' He drew nearer. 'Are you sure there is nothing between you?'

'Is it any concern of yours?' She saw that Carla and Brendan had gone on deck again, taking their drinks with them.

His eyes betrayed a sudden rush of feeling. 'He looks at you when you are unaware that he does so. He stays with you and your friends every time he can.'

'I can't stop him. He came with Brendan, and Carla likes Brendan, so we naturally spend a lot of time together.'

'Does he want you as much as I do, Samantha?'

She heard the water lapping along the hull and the gentle flap of the murmuring burgee at the head of the mast. The sun made a pattern of light through the elongated windows and fell on the back of Rhexenor's hand, turning the fine hairs to gold. It was a strong hand, the hand that had helped her on board and the hand that had held her waist in the dance. She recalled the light and potent kisses he had brushed along her arm and she trembled. He gently took her glass and put it on the table. From the upper deck came the sound of muted voices and laughter, and they were alone.

He came to her with all the grace of the god he resembled, and she was held close to his near-naked body. She knew every line of his tense well-muscled thighs and was conscious that she was wearing only a bikini and a thin cotton skirt.

His lips were cool and salty and firm, and instinctively, she put her fingers deep into the thick curling hair at the base of his skull. Breathlessly, she pushed him away as desire grew, appalled at her wanton response and blushing deeply. He gazed at her with awe. 'I didn't believe it possible,' he said. 'I want you, Samantha. I haven't looked at a woman for two years, and I want you.'

'No, Rhex, be sensible. It means nothing.'

He came towards her again but the voices on deck were nearer, 'You must come with me on the *Turtle*, just the two of us.' Panic filled her, mixed with her own desire. If she came to him on the boat, there could be no denying their needs. He would take her and she would belong to him, even though she knew he would never marry her.

In the depths of her mind, she remembered Max, the man who had tried to rape her. She remembered his rough passion and the terrible sensation of being forced to submit to a man's lust. She had been saved by his drunken weakness, but this was different. This time, a beautiful, powerful man would take her with her consent, and she would be lost for ever. 'I want you. I want you...' he whispered.

'Is there no wind? Aren't we going to sail?' asked Carla.

Rhexenor smiled with a wicked glint in his eyes. He took Samantha on deck with all the disinterested politeness of a guest taking tea with a dowager duchess and showed Brendan where to find the sails. The bright blue glistened as the sail billowed and the catamaran left her mooring. The wind came like a sailor's dream to send them singing over the waves, and Samantha knew real happiness in the rush of the white wake that cut through the blue sea. Even if he was totally devoid of morals, he wanted her as a woman, and she could take that memory with her long after Corfu was a warm dream of sunlight and blue skies. The radio crackled. She went forward to tell

Rhexenor, and he swung down into the cabin. He spoke in rapid Greek and listened. He made a note on a memo pad and spoke again, his face stern. The operator ended the call and Rhexenor walked slowly back on deck, frowning.

'What was that? A weather forecast?' asked Brendan.

'No, I have a friend who asks for my help sometimes. He is in Greek customs and watches boats that drop drugs for collection and distribution to mainland Greece. He asks me to look out for a certain boat that may cross these waters today or tonight.' He smiled at the solemn faces. 'So you do a good turn for the Greek government, coming out with me today. If I had not taken the boat, he could not have contacted me except at Afionis, by radio.'

'Where is it coming from, Rhexenor?'

He shrugged. 'Who knows? There are many countries with men willing to traffic in death, and these seas cover many routes. The boats are always as fishing boats but with powerful engines.' He laughed. 'They aren't here yet so we still have time for the sail.' He took the helm from Brendan and came closer to the wind, making the *Turtle* hurl through the water with air under one hull. It was exciting and reckless – as our love would be if I went to him, thought Samantha. She heard him laugh, saw the almost boyish glee when he thought of chasing smugglers and realised that he had switched away from her completely, as if he had never whispered 'I want you.'

And tomorrow when he went back to Afionis, would he whisper 'I want you' to the lovely Cassiami, or did he already know her more intimately? Did he hold her in his arms in the soft Greek nights? Samantha hid her humiliating thoughts, and the thrill of the fast boat made her smile again. This moment was good, whatever the future might not hold for her. I feel alive and desired, even if I have to go back alone and take second best in life, she told herself.

Twice the radio gave the call sign to *The*

Flying Turtle and Rhexenor made notes on a chart. The weather forecast came and he squinted up at the sun.

'Not good,' he murmured.

'Not good? It couldn't be better. Just look at that sky. Not a cloud in sight,' said Brendan. 'Are the forecasters any good?'

'Usually, but I hope they are playing safe because of all the holiday sailing boats in the area.' He shrugged. 'We'd better get back and drop you off in case I have to go out again.' Carla groaned. 'I have to see my dog, too. Eva is not good with him and he escapes.' He looked at Samantha. 'Will you look after him if I have to sail again? I must fill the fuel tanks and find Stavros, who comes with me sometimes.'

They took their time along the coast, and as if to contradict the weather men, the wind dropped, leaving a slight swell on the dark blue sea. They went back on power and tied up. A bark of welcome came from the taverna and Ariel swam out to the incoming dinghy, to come with it to the shore.

'I'll ask Eva for some packed food,' said Samantha. 'You might need it if you leave in a hurry and have to stay out there.'

He touched her hand. 'Thank you.' He was serious. 'You will look after my dog?' A sudden fear made her catch her breath. He forced a smile. 'I am not going to drown,' he said. 'Poseidon has no need of me. But I might be delayed.'

'I'll look after him,' she said. 'And – take care.'

He hurried away, and she put Ariel on a leash until he disappeared into the garage to find Stavros. Eva was waiting and almost ran to give orders for a basket of food to be prepared for Kyrie Gaia for the picnic on the boat, as she said in a loud voice so that none of the guests would speculate about the turn of events.

Ariel was restless and Samantha took him along the shore for a walk after lunch. They walked as far as the headland and sat in the shade, the dog panting and hot. He seemed to sniff the air nervously, and on the distant mountain Samantha saw the first flash of lightning. The dog whined and stirred and she put him back on the leash, frightened that he might run off into the trees and get lost. The air was heavy and the birds silent as they waited to find what Athena had planned for them. There was the smell of silent fear in the hot stones and she walked back, perspiring and suddenly depressed, and locked Ariel in Rhexenor's room.

'Did you see the lightning?' asked Carla.

'It was far away in Albania,' said Samantha. 'They might be having storms, but it doesn't mean we shall have one, too. Albania is miles. away across the strait and the sea is dead calm here.' She stretched out in the hot sun and watched the fast disappearing dot on the horizon that was *The Flying Turtle*, almost hidden from view now there were no sails flying. 'Not enough wind for sailing, and hardly enough to breathe. It's stifling,' said Samantha. 'It would be heavenly at Afionis now. If there is any breeze at all, the villa would catch it.'

'I'd like to be on the terrace where we had the party,' said Carla.

But Samantha was dreaming of an inner room, a room opening on to a cool court-yard where the sound of water cooled the mind and the fragrant green bushes cooled the air. It was his secret place where no strangers were admitted. Instinctively she knew this to be true and wondered why she had been shown that inner sanctum. Did Rhexenor take every pretty woman visitor to Afionis to the room, knowing that he wouldn't be disturbed and that the magic of the place could help him with his seduction? She moved and sat up as Iannis brought the Greek salad and bread, spreading a fresh table cover over the plastic table top.

Samantha was quiet all through lunch and Carla chatted to Brendan and left her to her thoughts. It was all so confusing. Rhexenor Gaia was attracted to her but held a low opinion of her, believing her to be an easy conquest for anyone seeking a brief holiday affair. He had to be polite to her because of her father, and so was a little more re-strained with her than he would be with a pretty girl he met casually. She pushed away her plate and sipped the coffee that she had allowed to become cold. It was bitter and she added sugar, but didn't drink it. He had said he wanted her, and the proof of that was there when she was held tightly to his body, his lips forcing her mouth into soft acceptance of his desire. She gazed out to sea, aware that her eyes were filling with tears. The dark glasses in her bag would hide her emotion. She fumbled through the assortment of tissues, sun-cream and money, and her fingers touched a coin that seemed thinner and more irregular in shape than the ordinary Greek currency. She laid the ancient coin on her palm, the turtle glinting in the sun, and looked out to sea again. The horizon was clear and there was no boat on the wide sea. She clenched her hand round the old coin and it seemed to bring Rhex nearer. The sky had lost its innocence across the water, and over the mountains of Albania mild flashes of light licked the peaks. The distant rumble of thunder made the stillness of the air even more oppressive, and many of the guests at the taverna decided to swim.

Samantha strolled back to the villa she shared with Carla. The small main street was empty and the heat shimmered over the scrubland along the shore. Ariel whined gently as she passed under the balcony of Rhexenor's room in the taverna, but made no fuss and seemed content to lie in the shade on the cool tiles, panting.

'I'll take you out later when it's cool, if your master doesn't come back,' she said. But he *will* come back. He must come back – he must be safe in that magnificent boat, she thought. Fishing boats lay on the sand, some on chocks as if stored for future use, and nowhere was there any activity. Nets lay to dry and the smaller boats were upturned as if to drain out storm water.

Hebe was sweeping the front of the café terrace. 'Why are the men not preparing the boats?' Samantha asked her.

'None go fishing,' said Hebe firmly. She looked up at the sky. 'It is bad for the sea. Nobody goes today or tonight.'

'But it's very calm. Do you think the storm over there will come here?'

'It will come and the wind will come *swoosh*. Only men like this–' she tapped her head to indicate no brains '–only they will sail now.'

'But Kyrie Gaia is sailing.'

'It is not good,' she muttered, and went into the café.

'I don't know how you can walk in the sun,' said Carla. 'I shall stay here in the shade of the taverna for the rest of the day. It's good and quiet and as cool as I'm going to be anywhere. Any news from the big city?'

'I saw Hebe and she was muttering that no one in his right mind would go out in a boat today. It seems to be all right, but the locals ought to know.' Albania was half hidden in mist, through which tiny bolts of silver flashed as Mercury fled the mountain slopes and hid in the heavens from the crashing thunder that chased him through the skies. A solitary sail appeared from the misty horizon and Samantha stared at it through binoculars. Her heart sank. It was a fishing boat with red sails set. There *was* wind out there. She saw the tiny figures on the boat pulling in the mainsail, and the small storm sail flew taut before the wind. The sea had a dull, sullen look and the air menaced with hot breath as eddies of sand rose from the shore. Fascinated, the watchers were taken by surprise as the wind whipped up like a lashing flail and struck the sea and the fishing boat. The men struggled to bring in every shred of sail and the engine spluttered into life. The boat came hurtling back to safety, the burgees singing a wild song. The boat wallowed and surged forward, making for the nearest shore, regardless of whether it was near a village or a conventional moor-ing. It beached a few hundred yards along the coast and the angry sea beat heavily against the wall under the villa.

Eva was struggling with the huge glass shutters that fitted over the whole of the taverna, turning it into an indoor room. Sand filtered across the open café area, making a fine silvery-gold tilth and covering Eva's precious plants with dust.

The sea was dark blue-grey and angry as the wind moulded the surface into fantastic waves, and as she moved back into shelter before the rain came in drenching torrents, Samantha prayed that Rhexenor Gaia, the man she hated and loved, would be spared. She fingered the turtle coin as if it were a good luck charm, and then remembered the dog. She spoke to Eva, who handed her the key to the room with the balcony and seemed relieved that someone was willing to take responsibility for Ariel as she could never make him obey or understand her.

'Keep the key until he comes,' she said. 'Iannis will give you food for him when you want, and he can come here if you bring him.'

Slowly Samantha turned the key in the lock and heard the excited whimperings. The dog made a fuss of her and then tried to run out of the room. She put him on a leash and took him downstairs, wondering if the thunder was upsetting him, but he pulled her towards the streaming glass windows. He's looking for Rhex, she thought, and put a consoling hand on the bright fur.

'He'll be back soon,' she whispered. 'Oh, God, make him come back soon.' A cold band constricted her heart. What if he didn't come soon – tonight or ever? He had asked her to look after his dog; had he some premonition of evil?

The telephone rang with shrill abruptness. Eva answered it and spoke in Greek, her mood changing from casual interest through slight irritation to anger. She muttered what sounded like something rather rude, causing even Iannis to raise his eyebrows.

'Not bad news?' asked Carla.

'No, it is nothing. The woman at Afionis,

Cassiami, she rings to say the boat was seen off the north side of the mountain before the storm but has not arrived at the village below Afionis. She ask why it has not arrived, and I tell her to ask the storm, to ask the gods and to pray to Athena! She tells me I should have stopped him... Me, Eva, stop Rhexenor when he wants to do something? Ha! She is all sour that one, unless he is there. I think it is Afionis she wants.'

'She might get it, if she marries Rhexenor,' said Carla, watching Samantha as she spoke.

Eva shrugged. 'He needs a one who will care for him as she could not, but she is good to look on...'

The telephone rang again and Iannis took up the receiver. He spoke rapidly, and when he put the phone down he looked anxious. He spoke to Eva, who threw up her hands and looked as if she was on the verge of noisy tears.

'What is it?' said Samantha, the cold

feeling intensifying.

'It is *The Flying Turtle*. The Customs man, Leonadis, who is the friend of Rhexenor, he saw the boat too and thinks it went out to sea after a fishing boat.'

'And now?' Samantha listened to the howling wind outside and saw the darkness that had covered the bay hours before sunset.

'He does not know. The radio is silent.'

Brendan saw the sudden pallor under Samantha's tan and smiled. 'It's nothing to worry about. If Rhex is following a boat and doesn't want to be seen, he'd keep radio silence and Leonadis wouldn't be able to contact him, nor would the fishing boat be sure of his position.'

'A fishing boat with radio? Is that usual?'

'If it's the one he thinks it is, Rhexenor won't be following a simple fishing boat but a boat that looks like one, with radio, sonar and possibly guns on board.'

"Guns?' Samantha sat down heavily.

'Don't worry. He knows what he's about.'

He glanced anxiously at the leaden sky. 'If only this storm hadn't sprung up. I've never seen anything like it, coming out of a clear blue sky.'

The wind had settled into a steady force six blow, but the seas were heavy and white caps fretted the waves. The group of scantily clad holidaymakers shivered; those with rooms in the taverna went to get warmer clothes and some of the others ordered metaxa, the warming Greek brandy. Ariel settled down with his head on Samantha's foot. 'Can I get you something warm from your villa?' asked Brendan.

Samantha stared through the windows. 'I think the rain has stopped. I'll go and take Ariel. He might need to go out, then I can put him back in the room.' The dog ran happily by her side, needing only a light touch on the leash to guide him. Samantha let him follow her up the stairway and quickly selected a warm sweatshirt for herself and an anorak and took a sweater for Carla in case she was cold. The rain dripping from the roof was chilly on her arm as she went back down the stairs, and the air was very much colder since the storm. She thought of the man on the catamaran, clad only in brief shorts, and tried to convince herself that he had warm clothes stowed away somewhere in the cabins. The food that she had suggested would be useful, at any rate, and she glowed with pleasure at the thought that she had made some contribution to his comfort. She took Ariel back to the room and made sure that the windows were shut fast. The dog settled down on his rug and she turned to leave.

A glint of metal caught her eye as she passed the dressing table. She picked up a coin that was exactly the same as the one she had in her handbag. She put it back and found her own. So Rhexenor Gaia had at least one of the coins. As she had done a hundred times, she wondered how the turtle coin had come to her father from the folds of tattered leather upholstery in the old Bugatti. A prickle of déjà vu made her hold both coins in her hand, together. If someone had lost the coin in the car, as she had lost her hair ribbon when she sat in Rhexenor's, the chances were that he or she was either a collector of coins or Greek.

'Be good,' she said to the dog, and put her own coin back in her bag. She could remember no Greek names among her father's racing companions, and he had never raced a car on Greek soil. So the link with Greece must be the buyer of the Bugatti. She took a deep breath and admitted the thought that she had refused to consider. It must have been Rhexenor who bought the car, and he would have gone to the house to see it and to talk about the restoration, the cost, the freightage and all the details that were necessary when an article was exported from one country to another.

Samantha gave the sweater to Carla.
'Is it still very rough?' Carla asked.
'The sea is terrible, but the rain has

stopped. I even saw a hint of sun trying to break through, so perhaps the worst is over.' Let him come back safely, she prayed.

The telephone rang and Eva almost ran to answer it. She came back agitated. 'What is it?' asked Samantha, through dry lips.

'Leonadis. He says the *Turtle* was sighted off the headland beyond the hidden rocks. The wind is driving down from the north and they are on the edge of the wrong shore. You know, they might be taken by the rocks.'

'Don't be frightened,' said Brendan. 'They have powerful engines and they both know what they're doing.'

'And if the catamaran goes on hidden rocks?'

'They would know about the rocks. They live here, remember. They have charts on board and sonar. They're safe unless they've lost power. The seas are far too heavy to sail, with that wind blowing. They tanked up with fuel and they had the engines checked this week. They must be OK.' And as he went on and on, Samantha wanted to scream, but we don't *know,* do we?

'I think I'll take Ariel as far as the headland. No, there's no need to come too. I'll take the glasses and if I see them, I'll wave my anorak. It's yellow and would show up well. You have some binoculars too, haven't you, Brendan? Keep an eye open in case the boat appears, and then Eva can get in touch with Leonadis.'

The road was entirely covered with muddy puddles, so Samantha decided she'd rather be clean wet if she had to be wet at all. She slung her sandals round her neck and rolled up the legs of the light cotton trousers she had slipped on when she went to fetch the extra clothes. She paddled in the shallow water and watched the white caps further out on the sea. The headland was still wreathed in light mist and she wondered if it was still visible from the hotel a mile on the other side. Perhaps even now, Rhexenor was drinking ouzo in the hotel bar or showering in the comfortable cloakroom that was often used by yachtsmen. She sent Ariel running ahead, and he threw a piece of stick in the air in his delight at being free again so soon. He ran towards a dark object that looked like a stranded porpoise, the loose folds of grey moving as the waves took it to and from the shoreline.

Samantha gasped. She walked more quickly, ignoring the possibility of spiny fish cutting her bare feet. She pulled at the limp rubber and managed to bring the stern out of the water where it was half submerged. The name was clear in the sea-washed rectangle of blue. *The Flying Turtle.* Sick at heart, she picked her way after the dog. Ariel stopped and lifted his head to bark. She could hear nothing but the waves and saw nothing but the grey sea and the spray on the hungry rocks. The headland emerged from the spray and she was breathing heavily. She went along the shore, convinced that she would make quicker progress on the firmer ground. The dog kept making small runs into the water as if trying to find courage to swim out to the rocks.

'Ariel,' she called, and she heard the echo of his name. She shivered. The wind was playing tricks – or Athena was in a mocking mood. She called again, and once more the dog's name was repeated. But it wasn't the echo of her voice. It was from a masculine throat, weary and distant as if the last of a considerable strength was exhausted.

'Rhexenor?' she shouted, and Ariel barked and scrambled over the rocks. 'Where are you?'

She went down to the headland and hardly felt the skin tearing from her feet as she walked over the sharp shells. 'Rhexenor?' She saw the mast of a boat and one shattered hull of the catamaran. On the rocks was a man, waving one arm feebly in the air. It was Stavros, and from the strange angle his left leg was assuming, he had broken it. 'Rhexenor?' she said, feverishly. Oh, God, let it be Rhex who was calling and not Stavros! He pointed and groaned. She saw a patch of sand on which a man lay, naked. The remnants of his torn shorts clung about his thighs like seaweed and blood was bright on his arm.

'Rhexenor...' He lay with eyes shut like a fallen Greek statue. 'Rhexenor, my darling. My darling,' she murmured, and cradled his head in her arms.

He opened his eyes and in their depths lurked the mocking insolence she remembered. 'Are you all right?' she asked, ashamed of her outburst.

'My Nausicaa... My princess,' he said, and lost consciousness.

7

'I don't believe you!' Samantha tossed back her long dark hair and glared at her father. 'You must have known I'd run into him sooner or later if he lived there. Why didn't you warn me?'

John Beauchamp raised his hands and let them fall as if words failed him. They had argued ever since Samantha had come from the airport, seething with inner rage. 'I knew him once, and yes, he was the man who bought the old Bugatti. How was I to know that you even remembered him? You were at school when he came here, about the time your mother died. I was too cut up to think of vintage cars, and he came back later, after a month or so.'

'Did he come the day of the funeral?'

John Beauchamp thought for a moment.

'Could be... He arrived and wanted to make an offer for the car and realised that it was no time for business. He stayed at a hotel for a couple of nights and went back to Corfu.' He smiled. 'I've met so many people interested in cars. I can't remember them all, Sam.'

'He remembered you, and because of that he had to be a little more polite to me than he might have been to just any girl on holiday. He didn't actually force me into bed!'

John raised an eyebrow. 'Don't get so worked up. If you hate him so much, fine! Forget him. If he was like that, I'm sorry, Sam. I had no idea he still lived there. But cool it, for heaven's sake. I've got people coming this evening.'

'I'm going out,' she said.

'I thought you'd be too tired after the journey. They are expecting to see you, Sam.'

'Who are they?' she said rudely. 'Business friends you could entertain at the local just as easily as here?'

'Sue said she'd look in to see if you were back, and a couple of the lads. There might be six altogether, and Sue is bringing the food already prepared, so there's nothing for you to do.'

'Quite a party! But I don't think you'll miss me. I'll go over to see Jan and then have an early night. You're right about me being tired.' She sighed. 'I have a lot to do tomorrow. I have to go up to London and put my name down with house agents.'

'I hoped you'd forget that idea, Sam. But please yourself. If that's what you want, go ahead.' He spoke mildly, with none of the heat that he had displayed each time she mentioned the possibility of having a place in London and a job there – a life of her own after caring for him for so long. She glanced at him with suspicion. He looked younger, less discontented. Perhaps the separation had been good after all and he had thought about the situation objectively while she was away.

'I'll ring Jan, and meet your friends,' she said. If he could make an effort to meet her on her terms, she could be generous too.

'And tomorrow, you'll tell me exactly what *did* happen in Corfu,' he said firmly. 'I hate to see you miserable, Sam, and I know that someone or something has made you very unhappy, even though you look better than I've seen you for a long time.' He looked with amazed approval at the pretty dress she was wearing and the feminine sandals with the thin straps that showed off her delicately arched feet. 'No garage work for you in future, Sam. I prefer the pretty girl in a becoming dress to the pump attendant in jeans that used to be around here.'

'I needed the disguise,' she said. 'But I think I can handle most situations now.'

'So he did try something and you smacked him down? Good girl.' He smiled. 'Can you handle Max? He's done nothing but ring to see when you're coming back.' She stiffened and her face was tight. 'Now don't be too hard on him, Sam. He's damned sorry about – that, and I've told him where he gets off.'

'He's not coming here tonight?'

'I haven't invited him,' said her father, but his eyes refused to meet her steady gaze.

'I hope he doesn't come,' she said, 'or I shall walk out on all of you. I thought I'd made it clear what I think about him.' She went to the office to use the telephone and, after two attempts to ring her friend Jan, she sighed and hung up the receiver. Even Jan was deserting her.

Her luggage was in her bedroom and she unpacked, putting her new clothes away carefully. She smoothed the creases from the coffee and cream dress that she had worn in Corfu and hung it away, not ready to wear it with anyone but the people with whom she had shared the most important time of her life. Sadly, she sat staring into space as she recalled the events following the day of the storm.

She could almost smell the salt water in the

man's hair as she bent over him, wrapping her warm sweat-shirt round his shoulders, and her own salt tears dropping on to his face. It had been a nightmare. The wind still howled and Ariel tried to lick the face of his master, getting in the way and dragging the sweater away from him again as fast as Samantha tucked it under him. She ran to the highest point of the headland and waved her yellow anorak so that Brendan would know that she had found something.

The mist was swirling along the beach, driven by the wind, which was clearing it from the other side of the rocky peninsula on which *The Flying Turtle* had foundered. Brendan couldn't see the headland, but someone from the holiday hotel saw her waving and having been alerted by Leonadis that a wreck might be sighted, rang him to bring an ambulance in case it was needed. Within minutes, help came from the other direction and Samantha watched the ambulance coming as close as it dared to bring stretchers for the injured men.

'How many?' asked the man she learned was Leonadis, the Customs officer. 'Please keep away and ask no questions,' he said to the small group of people running towards the scene from the hotel.

'Just Rhexenor Gaia and Stavros from the garage. He's over there with a broken leg, I think.'

Leonadis took over completely, and the two men were taken to the hospital in Kerkira. Samantha watched helplessly as Rhexenor was taken from her, without being able to speak to him again.

'I'll be in touch,' said Leonadis. 'I have to get them to the hospital and make sure that they speak to no one until I have learned all they have to tell me.'

'But he's unconscious. I want to go with him.'

'You would be...?'

'I found them!'

'I know, and I'm sure they will be very grateful, but please tell me who you are and I can pass on the information. You are one of the guests at the taverna?'

'Yes. I am living in Eva's villa. I am Samantha Beauchamp.'

Leonadis looked down at Ariel, who was whining at the closed door of the ambulance. 'If you could take the dog, Miss Beauchamp, that would help.'

She stared after the retreating vehicle. I can look after the dog! I am only a woman here on holiday who happened to be here and see the two men. I am nothing more.

Weary and footsore, she picked up the dog's leash and walked back to the village. She hardly noticed the pain in her feet or the blood that oozed from cuts on her toes.

Eva greeted her with dismay and sat her down with the first really hot coffee that Samantha had drunk in the taverna. Her teeth were chattering with cold and fatigue as she told Eva what had happened. Iannis brought a bowl of warm water and Carla bathed her cut feet, pulling two spines from the under-part of her right foot and stinging them with undiluted antiseptic.

'I'll put her to bed,' she said. 'Can you make the stairs if Brendan helps you, Samantha?'

She was dimly aware of two policemen in grey uniforms sitting listening, but it didn't register until she was in bed. 'Why the police?' she asked Carla when she was comfortable.

'They caught the men in the fishing boat. They had to give themselves up as their boat came in a hundred yards from the jeep in which the police were waiting and watching the sea.'

'What did they carry? Did they say?'

'They wouldn't talk much, but they had to telephone to Leonadis, and Brendan caught the word for gun.'

Samantha saw again the blood on Rhexenor's arm and head. And now he was unconscious! He might die, and they wouldn't let her near him. She was only a tourist with no rights to see him.

'I'll wait until they've gone and ring the hospital to enquire about Rhex and Stavros.

After all, we *are* more than guests here. We have been entertained by him and we have been on the boat,' Carla said.

'You wouldn't believe the boat, Carla. It's a wreck. The dinghy came ashore along the beach and seems to be punctured. It was flabby at one end and totally deflated at the other. Do you think they were shot? Promise me you'll come in even if you think I'm asleep and tell me what's going on?'

'I promise.'

But when Carla came to the villa, late that night, she shook her head. 'Stavros is sitting up in plaster but Rhex is still in theatre having a slug taken from his head and some more from his arm.' She handed Samantha some lotion for her cuts. 'Put some more on tonight and leave your feet free of dressings and they should heal quickly.'

'They're fine. They've stopped hurting already, and it's only when I walk that I feel anything. If I wear toeless sandals for a day or so, I shall manage very well.'

Carla paced the room restlessly. 'Stay in

bed until I call you in the morning in case you want help down the stairs,' she said.

'What are you trying to say, Carla? You've done nothing but evade my questions about Rhexenor. How badly injured is he?' Samantha was pale and, under the bedclothes, her hands twisted together in an agony of fear and uncertainty. He *must* live... He *must* get better... The thought of Rhexenor, with his enormous vitality and virility being dead or reduced to a vegetable was beyond belief.

'He's going to be all right, as far as they can tell. He has such strength, Sam, such reserves of sheer animal strength that he has to get over this.' She gazed out at the wild sea. 'If he doesn't get completely well, I think he'd rather be dead.'

Samantha turned her face to the pillow and wept. 'He should never have gone out. He knew that the storm was coming.'

Carla put a comforting hand on her shoulder. 'There's nothing we can do about it, honey. And to think that at one time I thought that he fancied you.'

'What do you mean?' Samantha brushed away the tears.

'Well, even that seems all sewn up. Cassiami was at the hospital telling everyone that she was in charge of the villa at Afionis and hinting that she would soon be the mistress of the whole estate, that they planned to marry soon.' Carla looked embarrassed. 'I know how you feel, honey. You were getting a bit too involved with that sexy hunk of man, weren't you? I warned you to look for a holiday whirl that wouldn't leave you panting. Better stick to Ben – he really is nuts about you. He wanted to come up here, but I said you might be asleep. I can call him if you like.'

'No, I don't want to see him. He's a very nice man and I'm glad I met him, but just now... No, Carla, keep him away if you can and try not to leave us alone. I can't get really enthusiastic about him and I want to get on my two feet and go to see Rhexenor as soon as possible, if only to say goodbye before we go back to England.' She smiled faintly. 'Or should I say before *I* go back. I just feel that we came together.'

'I shall be leaving soon, too.' Carla blushed. 'I might as well take in some of Europe while I'm this side of the pond. Brendan said he'd like me to stay with his folks for a few days, so I may see you in the U.K.'

'I'd like that. Can you stay with us, too? Come to us after you leave Brendan, and I can meet you at the station if you let us know the date of your arrival.'

It wasn't much, but it cheered Samantha to think that all links with Corfu wouldn't be broken so soon. The fact remained that she had only a few days before returning on her booked flight to England, the garage and her father – and to face life without Rhexenor Gaia, the man who was more to her than anyone she had met. In her heart she knew that he could take her and use her and go back to his olive trees and build a future with Cassiami, but after kissing his pale face and seeing the blood on the sculptured curls, she knew that she would be content with the merest crumb of his love if she could just see him with the old arrogant, appraising insolence in his eyes once more.

During the night she heard a dog howling and prayed that it wasn't Ariel howling for his master. She shivered, remembering the saying that dogs had a seventh sense that told them of impending doom and the coming of death, and could hardly restrain herself from getting dressed and creeping to the telephone in the taverna to ring the hospital. But she knew that it was impossible. She tried to ignore the strange murmurings of the sea outside her window and snatched at what little sleep came her way.

Carla tapped lightly on the door at eight and Samantha was already dressed and outwardly calm. Her feet were much better, thanks to Carla's soothing lotion, and she found that if she wore strappy sandals, she could walk fairly well with no pressure on the worst of the cuts. Almost defiantly, she had dressed to look her best, in a pleated cotton skirt of rainbow colours. What had Rhexenor said – the fig wore a close-fitting skin like the pale green tee-shirt she sometimes wore? She put it on, and the green echoed one of the many colours of the skirt. It fitted tightly, showing her curves and suggesting the voluptuous but taut figure beneath the clothes. Her tanned skin looked glossy and smooth and she clipped a thick gold bangle to her wrist.

Carla smiled with relief. 'I half expected to see you with rings under your eyes, but you look superb.'

'I'm going to the hospital, whatever they say,' said Samantha. 'So if you want to come, try to leave the men behind. Or shall I go alone?'

'Do you think you should?'

'I have every excuse, even for a tourist who happened to be in the same taverna,' she said bitterly. 'I left my sweat-shirt wrapped round his chest and I can ask if it's there ready for me to collect.'

She drank strong coffee and orange juice but ate nothing. Eva was fluttering round like an oversized dragonfly. 'You should eat, Miss Beauchamp. You have the shock but it is better now,' she wheedled.

'I thought you called me Samantha, and I am better,' she said. 'I'll be all right tonight to take Ariel for a walk, but I don't think I'd be able to go on the beach with him. I expect one of the men will take him this morning.'

It worked out as she wanted. Brendan and Ben both volunteered eagerly, and as soon as they had gone out of sight with Ariel, Samantha and Carla got the car. Carla drove to Corfu town, while Samantha's sore feet rested on the back seat. The sky was clear, as if Athena had changed her mind about blowing Corfu from the face of the earth and was smiling again. White-topped waves were still flecking the sea, but the sky was blue and the mist on the horizon was from heat and not heavy weather. With cooler air, freshened by the rain, it could have been a pleasant journey, but Carla didn't care for driving, and Samantha was on edge wondering if she would see Rhex or if the authorities would forbid it.

At last, they parked by the main entrance and walked slowly to the reception desk, where an elderly man who spoke very little English was sitting. Carla managed to make him understand that they wanted to fetch something from Kyrie Gaia's room that the English lady had lent him at the scene of the accident and, yes, they were friends. Yes, they had visited him at Afionis. It was a very fine villa and he was a very fine man, with, yes, many olive trees.

'Smile, Sam, he's letting us go up,' said Carla in English. 'Come on, before he changes his mind.'

They smiled at the man and thanked him effusively, and made for the stairs. Once round the corner, they ran so that he couldn't reach them without leaving his post.

'I'll wait by the door and stall anyone who comes. It might give you a minute if we really aren't allowed in,' said Carla.

'Bless you. I don't know how I'd have coped with him. I feel ashamed that I know so little Greek.'

They approached the door with number five on the thick dark wood. There was no notice on the door-handle, and Carla whispered that Samantha should open the door a little and peep inside to make sure that they were alone. 'But hurry, I feel like a criminal. I wonder if Greek hospital sisters are as formidable as some I've met at home?'

Samantha opened the door and saw a starkly white bed below the window. Rhexenor Gaia lay like a knight carved in stone on a tomb, with his head bandaged and his arm in plaster. The white coverlet did nothing to destroy the illusion of sickness, or worse, and she was almost overcome by the similarity to the scene when her father had returned from the operating theatre after his racing accident.

Taking her courage in both hands, she advanced to the bedside and looked down at the strong, noble face with the closed eyes. 'Rhex, can you hear me?' she whispered. 'Rhex, my darling, please get well.' Of course he couldn't hear, but one eyelid fluttered and the firm lips relaxed a little. 'Rhex.' She put a hand on his good arm. 'I know you can't hear me, but I have to say it just once. I love you. I know that you are to marry Cassiami and I wish you all happiness. Goodbye, my darling.'

She stumbled to the door, tears threatening to blind her.

Carla was talking to a nurse in a long white apron who seemed confused. 'Ask her about my sweat-shirt. That will explain why we're here,' said Samantha in a slightly shaky voice. Carla spoke again, and the nurse smiled and beckoned them to an office along the corridor.

They followed, and from the tail of her eye, Samantha saw another woman go into the room she had just left. The nurse reappeared, holding a bag in which the sweater reposed, and the hospital quiet was broken by the sound of a woman calling. The nurse ran to the room and Samantha followed. Cassiami was standing by the door, calling for the nurse. Through a crack in the door, they could see Rhexenor trying to sit up, muttering in a mixture of English and Greek.

'Why are you here?' asked Cassiami coldly.

'We came to fetch some things,' said Carla, with the air of one who does not expect to give an account of herself. 'And to see how Rhexenor is progressing.'

'He is having no visitors but me,' said Cassiami firmly. 'He is very ill and wants no one but me.'

'What was he saying?' asked the nurse, in Greek. 'You must tell me, Kyria. I have to write down everything he says.'

Cassiami glared at Samantha. 'You can see how ill he is. He talks of Nausicaa, the princess of Corfu who perhaps was never here.'

'He talked of her to me at the villa,' said Samantha.

'It means nothing, a trick of his mind. He is sick in the brain and I shall look after him when he comes home to Afionis.' The woman was smiling as if well pleased at the thought of having a man with an injured mind in her care.

She's telling me that he belongs to her and she will keep him from any outside influence, thought Samantha.

'If you have what you came to take, goodbye. I must sit with Rhexenor and care for him.' She went into the room and closed the door. As the heavy door swung to, it was the door of fate slamming in her face, and Samantha turned away, helpless and furious.

'If she has her way, it'll take the CIA to get through her guard in future,' said Carla. 'Come on, Sam. It's as well to know when you're beaten. Cut your losses and settle for what offers.'

'If you mean Ben, I'm afraid it's no. I want

to go home, Carla. I need time to think and get this terrible, magic place out of my heart.' The pain was turning to numbness. It was all a dream, the meeting with this wonderful arrogant man, his amused contempt for her and then the fact that, although he was going to marry Cassiami, he desired the girl he lightly called Nausicaa, the princess of the palace of Alcinous. A holiday romance, perhaps, but to her a fairy tale which would live in her heart long after she had left Corfu and the man she had tried not to love.

As Samantha put first the shorts and tee-shirts away and then folded the dresses, she came across the vivid kaftan she had worn in the café. Under the light in her room it lay like a fugitive rainbow, and with an air of decision, she draped it in front of her. When she had showered, she put it on, wondering if it still looked as good as it had under the blue skies of Corfu. She brushed her hair hard until the ends sprang up with electric impulses and shone blue-black in the mirror. It helped to know that she was looking her best, and she went downstairs feeling in control of herself, her emotions and her future. I must be hard; I must learn to use people and not to be used, she told herself. Even the conviction that one of the guests would be Max, whatever her father had said, did nothing to dent her new-found calm.

It didn't matter. Nothing mattered except for the empty space fast filling with brittle ice in her soul. She smiled brightly at Sue, an old friend of the family who was equally at home with Samantha and her friends and the car rally boys and the men from her father's racing days.

'Good to see you again, Sue,' said Samantha.

'I hope you didn't mind me bringing a few things. I know what it's like coming back and having to start right away. I thought it would give you a gentle beginning.'

'Thanks, Sue!' Samantha laughed. 'Not

that I'm all that fragile after a fortnight in the sun, but I can't say I'm dying to work here again.'

'John told me you wanted to work in London.'

'I think it's time I did. He doesn't need me now and I ought to be independent again.'

Sue nodded, and Samantha wondered why she didn't protest that John would miss her far too much if she went away permanently.

'The others should be here soon. I'll disappear into the kitchen for five minutes while you set out the drinks trolley,' said Sue.

'As if she was used to it,' murmured Samantha thoughtfully.

The door bell rang and she heard John's voice welcoming a couple whom she liked. She stepped forward into the hall and smiled. 'Hello, John didn't say that you were coming.' For the first time she slipped into calling her father by his first name, as he had asked her to do, many times. He

226

glanced up, pleased, as if he hoped for a new relationship between them. 'Come in, Sue is deep in the kitchen and I'm in charge of drinks.' Again, her father smiled with relief. He went to the door again and Samantha took the first of the guests into the sitting room.

'You look absolutely stunning, Sam,' said one of her father's old friends from the racing pits. He looked almost afraid of the new Samantha, and she noticed with a slightly bitter smile that he made no crude jokes while she was in the room. The hard shell seemed to be working, giving her a power that she never knew she possessed, and when Max strolled in with a self-satisfied glint in his eyes, she nodded to him coolly, as if she was expecting him and viewed him with all the lack of interest a vegetarian would show for a pound of sausages. She turned away and continued her conversation with a client of her father's, sensing the appraising glance that Max couldn't hide. So many things were now clear to her. She could live, if it was really living, without Rhex, without a heart but with a sharp knowledge of other people and what made them tick.

Her father joined her and touched her arm. 'You look wonderful, Sam. *Samantha*.'

She looked round the now crowded room. 'I thought you said half a dozen. This is a real party. What are we celebrating, John? Or is it a secret?'

He reddened. 'What do you mean?'

'Come off it, John. It's obvious. I can't say I'm surprised, but what took you so long? I like Sue and I hope you'll be very happy.'

'You don't mind? She made me promise to say nothing until I was sure you knew and that you were happy for us, so we made this your homecoming party.'

'No need. I'm not really coming home, am I? I'm a bird in flight, with no nest of her own.' She laughed. 'Tell the world, John, and I'll be the first to kiss the bride.' It was easy. There was no reason why she should object to her father marrying the woman who had loved him for so long and been content to remain a friend while Samantha looked after him. It didn't matter because she wouldn't be there, she'd be living in a soulless apartment in London, existing from day to day, dreaming from night to night and building up a barrier to protect her from ever being hurt again.

'I think John has something to say,' she called, during a lull in the conversation, and stood smiling in her beautiful long dress while toasts were drunk and congratulations filled the air.

Max came to her side. 'Am I forgiven?' he asked fatuously.

She frowned as if trying to remember. 'For what?'

'You don't want me to spell it out, do you?'

'I don't want you to do anything, Max. The drink is over there, the food is on the table. Feel free. Be yourself, but please excuse me, I'm very busy.'

Someone called Samantha to the telephone. 'Samantha Beauchamp here,' she said.

'It's Ben. I happened to be in your part of the country and I wondered if I could see you. I've just arrived back from Corfu.'

'Ben?' It was a voice from the forbidden past, whispering through the chinks of her mind. She recovered sharply. 'Where are you? We're in the middle of a party. Can you come over?'

'Great!' he said. 'I'm ringing from the corner near the garage! If you hadn't been in, I was going straight to the pub where I have a room booked for the night.'

She smiled slowly. Poor dear Ben. She opened the front door and saw him hurrying up the driveway. She asked him in and took his coat and hated herself for smiling at him as if she were delighted to see him.

'This is Ben – we met on holiday,' she said, as they entered the room.

John and Sue beamed at him, imagining that he might be the cause of Samantha's new prettiness. Max stared as Samantha put a hand lightly on Ben's arm and steered him round to be introduced. Poor Ben, she thought again; but goodbye, Max. She led him to a corner after he had helped himself to the seemingly endless supply of food.

'You look marvellous,' he said for the third time.

'So do you,' she said, with a smile. 'It's all that lovely sunshine.'

'I missed you,' he said. 'It wasn't the same after you left.'

'It wasn't the same after the wreck,' she said sadly. 'I wanted to leave and come home.'

'I came with Brendan, and Carla managed to get a seat on our flight. It was a bit sad leaving... Good vibes and memories,' he said, almost choking over canapé.

'It was good, Ben. I shall never forget Corfu as long as I live. I shall miss them all. How was Ariel? He must be confused by all the people taking care of him.' She couldn't force *his* name from her lips.

'The dog? Oh, I think he went back to Afionis. The Customs bloke took him – Leonadis – when he came to see Eva and ask Stavros a few more questions.'

'Stavros? Is he back at home? I thought he was in plaster.'

'He's lording it with all the local females and has put Iannis' nose out. They all think Stavros is a hero and hang on every word he says.'

'And what does he say? What happened in the catamaran to cause the accident?'

'That's all over, Samantha. I'd rather talk about you.'

'But I want to know. After all, I gave the skin off my feet for that good cause and I *did* find them,' she said, hoping that her interest would be taken for idle curiosity.

John and Sue joined them, and with an extended audience preventing the cosy chat with Samantha that he wanted, Ben warmed to the description of what had happened.

'Tell us, Ben. John and Sue are interested,

because John met Rhexenor years ago.'

'They started out just as the weather was breaking,' said Ben, with irritating slowness. 'The catamaran was in good condition because Stavros had seen to it and it had tanks full of fuel.' For goodness sake get on with it, Samantha wanted to say. I know all that. What happened to Rhex?

Ben looked at his empty glass and Sue took it from him. 'Thanks, Sue,' he said. 'Where was I?'

'They'd started out and gone round the headland where we couldn't see them and the storm broke. The fishing boat beat its way back to the shore and we lost track of *The Flying Turtle* because there was radio silence.' Samantha rushed through the bits she knew about and hoped that Ben would go on from there.

'I'd forgotten that you knew so much about it, Samantha. Thanks Sue.' He took a long pull at his beer and stuffed his mouth with pâté sandwich. 'These are good. Did you make them, Sue?'

'For crying out loud, can't you get on with it,' Samantha whispered, and only John heard her. He glanced at the two pink spots appearing on her cheeks and knew that his daughter was under some kind of stress. She sat, unnaturally silent, her eyes filled with sadness.

'The storm got worse and they sighted the second of the fishing boats. They used one as a decoy – the one we saw come in, or rather, you all saw it but I was in Corfu. By the way, thanks for the use of the car. It made all the difference to my work.' It looked to Samantha as if he might go off on a tangent and talk about the history of the Church of Strangers or some other vital subject.

'Come on, man, don't keep us in suspense. I'm very concerned about Rhexenor,' John interrupted, and Samantha shot a look of pure gratitude to her father.

'The second boat had the lot – the drugs, really powerful engines and a gun mounted under the fishing nets. They fired at the boat when they saw it following and got the dinghy first. Stavros said it was useless and holding back the catamaran, so he slashed the rope towing it and let it go. The catamaran was gaining as she too has good engines and they fired again, ripping one float and the rudder and causing the boat to slew over on one side.'

'And Rhexenor?'

'He tried to bring the boat round but it was wallowing helplessly. The engine wasn't enough to keep her steady and they headed straight for the rocks. Stavros got gashes and a broken leg trying to jump for the shore, and Rhexenor was hit twice by flying bullets. He was flung on the shore by a huge wave, or he would certainly have drowned.'

'He said that Poseidon had no need of him,' said Samantha. 'I found them, and Leonadis took over and sent them to the hospital. So I took Ariel back to the taverna.'

'Ariel?' said Sue. She laughed. 'And was this Rhexenor a second Prospero?'

'Further back than that,' said Samantha. 'He was Odysseus.'

'You're right, Samantha. I shall use him as an illustration for my work on the tie-up between Shakespeare and Homer.' Ben smiled fondly. 'Bright of you to see the link. He is like the original, a fine-looking guy of that type.'

'And now? Is he recovering?' asked John.

'He went back to Afionis to be looked after by that gorgeous Greek woman. She's devoted to him and gets jealous if anyone offers to help. They'll be married as soon as he recovers.'

'Did he say so?' asked Samantha.

'Cassiami said so. He doesn't have visitors yet. They still have to take a bullet from his arm – they had to leave it when they worked on his skull. They did a decompression, which means that there was either a slug or a piece of bone pressing on his brain. Cassiami said that he was sitting up and taking notice when Eva telephoned just before we left.' Ben smiled again. 'No need to worry about him. With all the attention from a woman like that, he'll have no time to think of anything but getting better and making a new life with Cassiami.'

'Sounds as if she's got it all made,' said John.

'And she'll never let him go,' said Samantha.

8

Samantha examined her finger-nails. The well-shaped nails with perfectly applied varnish looked unfamiliar. It took a little time to get used to being a career woman who hardly ever soiled her hands except to do the normal chores of looking after one small, very smart apartment, and her general air of sleek well-being gave the impression that she was cool, professional, very beautiful and quite detached from the more human side of life. She sighed and looked out at the red creeper on the old building opposite the new apartment block. There would be red creeper all over the garage and the barn at the back where her father stored any old car on which he was working.

She read again the letter that John had sent her, and a pang of something bordering on envy gripped her as she sensed his happiness. There had been so much to do since she left home to take up her job in London that it seemed impossible that John and Sue were going to be married in one week's time.

'You are due for a little break by now, Samantha. We need you here for the wedding, and if you could just stay at the garage – no chores, I insist that this must be a holiday for you, but if you could keep an eye on things, I could go away for a week and feel free to forget the place knowing it would be in good hands. I shall ring on Sunday evening about ten. If you can't stay for the week, come for the weekend and I'll ask Don to get a friend in to help him as well as the lad I've already taken on.'

The telephone rang. 'I got your letter,' she said. 'I'll come to stay for the whole week. I feel I need a change and I've fixed it with my boss.' She laughed. 'At least I can sort out your books for you, but I promise I won't damage my newly-grown and elegant finger-nails on your behalf.'

She felt better after the call. London was lonely at weekends. The kind of man who asked her to dinner seemed to think that he was paying for a night's entertainment in her apartment, and when she told them simply that she didn't sleep around, they were shattered, found the barrier impenetrable and went away. She thought of Ben, who still tried to date her, but she couldn't be unfair and use him if she couldn't fall in love with him.

'I shall have a lonely old age – keep ten cats and do good works,' she told her very sophisticated reflection. She wondered if there was red Virginia creeper in Corfu, or if the land was becoming green with heavy rains. The women would be searching out their knitting needles to begin on the winter batch of woollens to be sold to tourists the next summer. How was Ariel? She tried to think of John and Sue, but the face that haunted her dreams and every moment of idleness during the day was beautiful, with a strong, chiselled jaw and deep eloquent eyes. Would this gnawing memory never leave her? She argued that he couldn't be as beautiful and that distance and the illusions gathered on holiday were coloured by the accident, making the whole unreal situation exaggerated. I didn't even like him half the time, she thought. But the other times? A shiver ran down her spine as she recalled the tender kisses on her wrist and arms, the rich deep voice that talked of Homer and the Palace of Alcinous and the heady sense of being hypnotised by desire when he showed her the meaning behind the ripe fruit of the fig.

She tore her thoughts away, frowning. John had talked of another man who would take on the garage work while he was away, and wondered if he would be efficient. John had also hinted that he was starting on yet another vintage car, which was a bargain and impossible to leave to a dealer. She smiled. Dear John... He had probably bought a rotting hulk which would disintegrate at a touch. She thought of the Bugatti that he had restored and the wonder of the fine car on the dusty roads of Afionis.

All thoughts led back there, to the man who was still an invalid, as far as she knew, being cared for by the jealous Cassiami. If he gets well, will he get married soon? Will the church bells ring for him and the tables under the olive trees groan with their burden of food and fruit and wine? Will he dance again, with all the passion of a man newly discovering love? She reflected that Eva was convinced that he had turned back to the world and its hopes and desires the night he danced in the café for her, in anger. Her breath quickened. He *had* wanted her. It didn't matter what happened now, he had wanted her, with all the fervour of a virile, perfect specimen of manhood.

The week passed slowly, but Samantha had time to look for something pretty to wear at her father's wedding, and she arrived at the house by the garage feeling that she would fulfil all the requirements for a dutiful daughter. The pale lilac pure silk suit, with bitter chocolate shoes and handbag, made her hair seem even darker and more luxuriant, and the tan that she had acquired in Corfu was still deep enough to make her appear smooth and leisured.

John greeted her with unconcealed delight, and it was impossible to be depressed having such joy around her. 'Come and see what I've got,' he said, wiping the oil from his hands.

'I thought you promised Sue on your word of honour that you'd give up greasing cars for at least three days before the wedding! And here you are, the day before the ceremony, with black finger-nails.'

'This is special. I had to coat some of it with grease in case it deteriorated before I come back. I have a client interested and I had to make a start on it.'

Samantha stared at the car in the old barn. Flakes of rust hung like some nasty skin disease from the coach work and the upholstery could have made a bird's nest for a whole family of eagles. 'Deteriorate? It's gone past that.'

'Rubbish! When I've finished with it, it will be worth a fortune. It's an early Bentley and the only one of its kind that I know of.' He looked inside the bonnet. 'Start her up, Sam.'

Samantha sat behind the massive steering wheel and moved it from side to side. 'A lot of play... You'll never get it right, John.'

'Start her up,' he repeated, lifting the shaky bonnet. 'We'll manage. You won't recognise it in six months' time.

She turned on the ignition, and John peered at the shuddering engine. He touched a lead and drew his hand back sharply. 'It needs time,' he said happily, 'and I shall be in no hurry to sell. I've three people interested who haven't even seen it.'

'Straight from a loony bin?'

'No, there's a member of the Japanese Embassy who wants to drive in the London to Brighton next year, an American, businessman who sponsors some car rallies and one other.'

Samantha saw him stiffen, as if bracing himself to tell her something she would hate to hear. 'The third, John?'

'My agent was talking to some of the Greek team and they mentioned that Rhexenor Gaia was better and needed something to interest him after the long spell in hospital.' John glanced up, his oil-streaked face oddly pleading. 'I know how he feels, Sam. It's hell to feel less than you are, even if you know you'll get over it.'

'He's better? Did you hear if he's being married soon?'

'No idea. My agent only talked about the car.' John pulled back the bonnet hood and went to look at the twin exhausts that were pushing out black smoke. 'Turn her off, Sam. She's a bit hot.' He wiped his oily hands on a piece of rag. 'This may be the last time I have to talk to you before the wedding, and then we'll be off before dinner tomorrow.' He looked at her keenly. 'What *did* happen in Corfu, Samantha? No, don't toss your head like that. I thought when you came back that you'd had an affair and quarrelled, until you told us about the shipwreck. You came back with a new prettiness – a bit like my Sue has now we're nearly married – it's a kind of glow, and to me it means that you are in love.'

'He wanted me, but he's going to marry Cassiami. You heard what Ben said about it.' She leaned forward over the wheel and her hair fell like a veil, hiding her face. 'Oh, Dad, they wouldn't let me see him. I sneaked in with Carla, but Cassiami saw us and made it quite clear that I wasn't wanted. She even told the hospital not to give anyone news but her, and when Eva rang, she told her that he was being transferred to Afionis as soon as possible and she would nurse him with the help of his housekeeper and living-in servants.'

It came pouring out, all the half-admitted misery that lay under her cool exterior. John put a consoling hand on her arm. 'Come on,

I'll get cleaned up and we'll have lunch. Promise me you'll do nothing daft, like marrying someone like Ben because you think you'll never fall in love again.'

'It would be less painful. A nice peaceful undemanding relationship with someone as good as Ben.'

'Since when have you wanted peace? It isn't you, Sam. Promise you'll make no decisions for a few months?'

'I promise. And forget me – this is your time for happiness, and I *do* wish you happiness.'

'One thing,' said John, as he poured sherry for her before they had lunch. 'Open all the mail and sort it for me. If there's a very good offer for the Citroën, sell it. You know the drill, and if anyone enquires about the Bentley, let them come and see it by appointment.'

She smiled. It was good to be treated as if she was as much an expert as he was, but she knew that he was doing his best to make her seem important. 'I might sell it for scrap,' she teased.

'You wouldn't dare, any more than you'd take a man unless you were crazy for him.' He looked at her over his glass. 'And when he comes, take what life offers, even if it sends you to the ends of the earth.'

'You want to get rid of me,' she said, with an attempt at a laugh. 'I'll get you two out of my hair before I think of running off with some new garage-hand. You might have chosen someone a little more appetising! I think you were leaving him as some kind of chaperone.'

They ate, and then had coffee while going over the papers and mail. The day passed quickly and to her surprise, Samantha slept deeply and woke refreshed for the wedding.

Even his hands were free of oil and John Beauchamp looked handsome and fit in the unfamiliar new suit and silk shirt. Weddings should always be like this, thought Samantha, full of lighthearted warmth, informality and the company of the friends the bride and groom really liked to have with them. In Corfu, the wedding would be more lavish. Would they follow the Greek custom of pinning paper money to the bride's dress? Hardly necessary for Cassiami when she marries one of the richest and most powerful men in Corfu, thought Samantha, then dragged her mind back to her duties as hostess and daughter of the groom.

The silk suit made heads turn and she was glad that it wasn't more elaborate. The last thing that Samantha wanted was to outshine the bride, but for John there was only one woman on this day.

Visitors came and went to view the wedding presents and to add their congratulations to the many cards and telegrams from all over the world. John was slightly bemused at the number of people who remembered him as a racing star. His agent had done well. There were newspaper articles in the national press and in racing magazines on the theme of recovery – from injury and from sadness. A team of television reporters came to the church and for a brief interview at the reception, insisting that Samantha should be included in photographs.

Max hovered on the edges and tried to get near Samantha, but she kept him firmly at arm's length and made it clear that she had no time for him. I wish I'd invited Ben, she thought. The loneliness of being a single woman among so many couples was becoming more than she could bear, and when John and Sue left, in a scattering of confetti – in a vintage car driven by a friend who persuaded John that it was the only way to travel to the airport – Samantha went back to the house and the quiet of the creeper-covered barn.

She walked into the huge high-ceilinged building and pulled the dust sheet from the old Bentley. She ran her fingers under the frayed sides of the upholstery, not really searching, but wondering if there would be anything as romantic as the old Greek coin she had found there.

As dusk came, she changed from her smart clothes into a simple shirt of broderie anglaise in soft pink, tucked into a skirt of burgundy velvet. She made coffee and went into the office to see if anything needed her immediate attention. The papers were muddled and she knew that it would take a couple of hours to sort out some kind of order before she could begin on them. She smiled. John's idea of a restful holiday wasn't exactly hers. She found the three letters concerning the old car, and was amused at the curious wording of the Japanese's effort. He certainly managed to put across the idea that he wanted the car very much and said some very flattering things about John's career. Her heart warmed to him more than to the American businessman, who wanted to put it on show in his car showroom. 'He could buy a fibre-glass model for that purpose,' she murmured, and resolved to let the car go to an enthusiast.

The dates were interesting. The Japanese gentleman wanted to come to see the car the next day. She glanced at the desk diary. Sue had entered his name for eleven a.m. She stared at the letter she had kept until last. It was typed by a secretary and was the formal suggestion that Mr Gaia would like to inspect the car. Her hand shook when she saw the scribbled entry in the diary. The day after tomorrow, at four p.m. *Please arrange a car to pick Mr Gaia up at the airport,* she read. Flight from Athens to Gatwick.

The new lad tapped on the glass panel of the office door. 'I've locked the pumps, miss, and the money is in the safe. See you tomorrow.'

'Wait... Do you know anything about a car for the airport on Wednesday?'

'Mr Beauchamp said you'd be arranging it, miss.'

'Oh, he did, did he?' said Samantha, grimly. 'Right, I'll get someone to do it.'

The boy lingered. 'I don't know who, miss. It's oil delivery on Wednesday and the rep

253

for soft drinks wanted to set up the new dispenser. Mr Beauchamp said we'd be needed here.'

'I'll think of something,' said Samantha.

A taxi? She chewed the end of a ball-point pen. The driver could miss him among the airport crowds and John would be annoyed if an important client was neglected, but her heart beat fast with a mixture of dread and longing. He didn't know that she was here, or he wouldn't have arranged to come. He knew her as a girl who enjoyed light romantic interludes with people like Ben, and who could be roused to indulge in passionate kisses with a man who despised her but desired her. It might be more tactful to send a car and let the senior garage man take all particulars and any offer he might care to make before driving him to his hotel.

But I must see him, her heart cried. Just once more before he marries Cassiami and goes out of my life for ever. I could send a car and just see to the business side, here. John would want me to feed him before he goes to a hotel. We always do when someone comes from a distance. She closed her mind to the fact that their hospitality went deeper, offering a bed for the night and a tour of the local beauty spots. Just what does John think he's done? she wondered. True, he had many matters on his mind and a man taking marriage vows wasn't likely to have his mind on dull business deals. But this was no dull business deal. She recalled his enthusiasm in the barn and knew that he must have received the letter before he showed her the old car.

If I sell the car to the Japanese, I can cable him as if the message comes from John and make him put off his visit, she thought. No, there might not be time and she might not sell the car. She would ring Ben! He would like to meet Rhex again, and it would save any embarrassment if she could hint that there was something lasting between her and the man she liked but did not love. She dialled the number that Ben had left on the pad in a conspicuous position. It rang and rang and she ached for him to answer, but only the mocking dialling tone reached her, and she remembered that he had said he was going to stay with the co-author of one of his historical books.

In the morning, the glossy magazine dealing with all aspects of car racing and rallying plopped through the office letter-box. In it was a brief run-down of John's career, with the promise of details of the wedding in the next issue. It mentioned several famous names among the interesting people who will be there, and added, 'and John's charming daughter, who gave up her career to nurse him after his accident and to whom he owes his recovery.' There was an out-of-date photograph of her in jeans and sweatshirt by the petrol pumps.

John must have given them the interview last week, she thought. There was a lump in her throat as she realised her father loved her enough to acknowledge that he knew he owed his recovery to her as well as to the surgeons who had repaired his damaged limbs. She put the magazine on one side and opened the rest of the mail.

Samantha wrote several urgent letters, then took them to the post office in the village, using a small car that was a family work-horse. On her return, she glanced at the clock and saw that she had just half an hour before the man from the Japanese Embassy arrived. She changed into the velvet skirt she had worn the night before and put coffee on to filter. There was cold chicken and salad in the fridge and lots of fresh apple pie and cream, trifles left over from the reception and brought back by Mrs Trent, the part-time housekeeper, together with cheese and savouries, as if someone was conspiring to make sure that she could feed any number of unexpected guests.

Mr Okawa was charming and very en-thusiastic. He climbed all over the car and sat behind the wheel. Samantha smiled as he took photographs from all angles and she offered, half in fun, to take a few shots of him by the car. He bowed politely and sat behind the wheel again, the glitter behind his well-polished spectacles giving the lie to the solemn expression on his face. Samantha gladly entertained him to lunch and heard about his family in Japan and his wife, who accompanied him on his tours of duty but didn't enjoy travelling.

It was tempting to say that he could have the first refusal of the car when it was restored, but she knew that this would be a coward's way out and she would be letting John down if she didn't at least pay lip-service to all the bidders. His offer fell short of the American one, and she hinted that she might have to persuade her father to reconsider the price he would accept. They parted on terms of mutual approval and he promised to send her one of the photographs of her by the car.

Two down and one to go, she thought, and tried to forget the ordeal ahead of her. She threw herself into her work and became engrossed in making order out of John's chaos. The house was tidy and homely, there was food for an army in the house and she sat watching a late play, wondering how to make the night longer, and how to put off the meeting that her heart yearned for. At midnight, she was arranging red Virginia creeper in low vases. At one, she drank coffee, and at two, she fell asleep in the chair, exhausted.

9

The second cup of airport coffee tasted even worse than the one she had drunk as soon as she arrived, but her mouth was dry and she had to do something while she waited for the Athens plane to land at Gatwick airport. She went in search of a toilet. She didn't know whether it was excitement, fear or coffee that made her want to visit a lavatory, but her faint panic was becoming an obsession. I'd be like this on my wedding day, she thought, but she couldn't visualise herself as a bride.

Weddings! She recalled the two happy faces at the altar when her father had married his Sue. Did the brides in Greece name the day and arrange the wedding, or were the men so chauvinistic that they said where the reception would be held and what the bride should wear? But Cassiami would want to have everything exactly as she wished. Samantha smiled faintly. It would almost be a relief to get the meeting over, to establish herself as her father's business partner and to keep everything on an impersonal level.

A month or so ago I didn't know he existed, and now I'm waiting here, much too early, for a man who will make me want to turn tail and run as soon as I see him – or make me want to fling myself into his arms and demand his love. My mind and heart were intact and I planned a career, I still want a career – The mangled voice of the announcer interrupted her thoughts, telling her that the flight from Athens was arriving. Samantha started up. Why Athens? Sue had written Athens on the pad, but shouldn't it be Corfu? He lived within driving distance of Corfu Airport. Had there been a mistake? She swallowed hard and went to stand by the barrier through which passengers would come from customs. I'll wait until the last passenger has gone and then enquire about planes from Corfu if he doesn't appear, she thought. The doubt was making her jumpy, just when she was priding herself on her coolness, dressed in the lilac suit, with her face made up discreetly and well.

In a few minutes, the air would be rent with the sound of his plane – if he was on it – and he would burst into her English existence. Would it be a shock to find that the man she worshipped as the most masculine and beautiful creature she had met was less than that, under the pale impersonal lights of the airport terminal? She drew back from the barrier. He wasn't expecting to see her, so she would have the advantage of seeing him first. It would be good to remain unobserved, to be able to look at him and convince herself that she no longer loved him. It would test her reactions to seeing him in her environment.

Scurrying figures came from another flight; Jamaicans coming from holidays in Kingston, from their own islands of sunshine, music and laughter. The growing chill of late English summer made them subdued, the children round-eyed and solemn, the parents sensing the stress of living far from their roots.

Samantha stood waiting, growing more and more apprehensive. Where was the man who had run along the white sand, nearly naked, with his dog completing the picture of perfect physical beauty? Would his brilliance fade under grey skies? A blur of faces spilled between stern uniformed men who scrutinised every passenger. A young girl rushed into the arms of a fair-haired student, his too-long arms opening to enfold her with poignancy and tenderness. Samantha looked away. The girl was bright-eyed and breathless with happiness, laughing and talking. They stopped to kiss before they reached the exit and a chill that had nothing to do with the warm afternoon made Samantha cold at heart.

Then she saw him. He was weary and looked slightly annoyed as he stood with his luggage and glanced around for a trolley. His hair was gold-tipped and his skin warm and suntanned. He was taller than she remembered. Two women smiled at him but he ignored them. Even away from paradise he was a god, and a rush of uncontrollable happiness flowed over her as she went towards him with the trolley she held ready for his luggage. It was enough to see him and to talk to him, even if only about her father's business.

'Hello, Rhexenor,' she said, and held out her hand.

'You?' He looked at the trolley. 'You are going away? Your father said you were in London.'

'Correction,' she said, with a smile. 'He has gone away and I am attending to his chaotic office while he's on his honeymoon.' He stared at her and she couldn't make out if he was annoyed or just surprised. 'So I am secretary, hostess and chauffeur. Your bags, Sir!' She picked up one case and swung it on to the trolley.

'I can do that. I still have one good arm.'
He took another case and put it on top of
the first and caught up two holdalls. The
brief contact of the casual handshake made
Samantha busy herself over the balance of
the trolley. 'I can manage,' he said.

'I'll push the trolley. Your arm must be
stiff.' She pushed, and the trolley went off at
a tangent, nearly colliding with another one
equally badly biased. He took one side and
she stayed on the other and slowly they
made their way to the car.

'I hope you drive better than you push
trolleys,' he said. 'I didn't expect to see you
here. Hello!' The sweetness of his smile left
her breathless. 'I'm glad your father sent
you.'

'He's sorry to miss you,' she began.

'Miss me? But I'm seeing him next week
after I've been to London.'

'You're staying?'

'You don't think I travel overnight with all
this luggage, do you? I have a lot of business
that I couldn't attend to since my accident

and I've come to clear it up.' He glanced sideways at her bright colour. 'Too much for you? We have no need to run, have we? I hate loose ends and I have a lot of things to do in England before I can give my mind to other matters.'

'How is Ariel?'

'Very well. He sends his salutations,' he said gravely. They laughed, breaking the tension between them. 'He was cross with me for leaving him again, but your laws are strict and even a good dog like Ariel is not allowed on your shores. Rightly, I hasten to add, but sad for all that.'

The trolley quickened and had to be held back as they went down the last ramp to the waiting car. Samantha unlocked the back and they thrust the luggage inside. Rhexenor sat beside her and she could smell the elusive scent of wild thyme on his clothes.

'Have you been staying in Athens? I began to wonder if I was waiting for the right plane,' she said, skilfully weaving between the badly parked vehicles and making for the airport perimeter.

'Cassiami had to go to Athens to stay with her brother,' he said. 'I took her there to make sure she got there safely. She is now in his care.'

'Male chauvinist you might be, but the Greeks look after their womenfolk,' said Samantha lightly. She waited at her junction and Rhexenor didn't speak until she was in the stream of traffic again.

'You look very well,' he said. 'I was surprised to see you at the airport. What are you doing? Living at home with John?'

'No, I have a life of my own at last. John is well and has no real need of me.'

'That I can't believe, even if he has married. I heard how you cared for him when he was crippled. I had no idea that you had so many attributes.'

He smiled, and his eyes held a hint of the humorous derision that she recalled so vividly. It was better that he looked at her like that and had no tenderness in his eyes. She sat straighter in the driver's seat. At least his voice held more respect now.

'He needed me, so there was nothing I could do but come home to care for him,' she said simply.

'He was fortunate. You were not there to look after me.'

'You had no need of me.' Her mouth almost refused to form the words. 'You had so many people anxious to look after you that there was no place for someone who just happened to be on holiday in Corfu for two weeks.'

He glanced at her sharply, but her driving discipline helped her to keep calm and concentrate on the road ahead. She passed a lorry, kept to the middle lane until she was clear of the convoy of three removal vans and regained the inner lane.

'I would like to have seen you to thank you for your help the day I was thrown on to the shore.'

'I did nothing. I merely alerted the hotel. They told Leonadis and he took over completely.' She held back all but a hint of bitterness. 'I was trusted to take Ariel to the taverna.'

'Yes, Leonadis told me.' He grinned. 'He will not forget the ravings of a madman.' She almost crashed the gears as she turned off into a service area. 'I learned what had happened and I was angry. I also learned from Eva that your feet were torn on the rocks when you came to help me.'

'That was my own fault,' she said. 'I had been warned often enough to wear canvas shoes while walking along the beach. I didn't think sufficiently.' She stopped the car. 'Would you like some coffee? I came away in a hurry to meet the plane,' she lied. They walked slowly to the cafeteria, the cool breeze fluttering the silk skirt and making it look like a falling rose petal. This was better. I'll take you in small doses, she vowed. The contact with his arm or leg as she changed gears or used the floor-mounted hand brake was too much for her peace of mind.

'This is almost as bad as Iannis' coffee,' he said, pushing away the dark brew and sitting back in the seat, watching her.

'Not a very good idea after all,' she said, finding his cool appraisal even worse than his nearness while she was driving. 'I'll make some good coffee when we get back.'

He raised an eyebrow. 'You are taking me to your home? With John away and no chaperone?'

'When a person is engaged to be married, surely there is little danger of any emotional entanglement,' she said, but her heart beat faster at the rashness of her invitation. 'I think that you are a man of honour, Rhexenor, and would never abuse the house of a friend.' Her lips curled slightly. He might try to seduce her on neutral territory, but his Corfiot breeding would prevail in his friend's house. He was engaged to Cassiami, and now that he was aware that this was common knowledge, he couldn't make advances to another woman. He had said to her on *The Flying Turtle* that he would feel insulted if any woman felt safe with him on his boat. She looked out at the heavy green of late summer with the first tinges of red and gold in the trees. This was a colder country and a saner one. Here she could fall back on the old conventions that had sometimes seemed irksome, but which now gave her safety if she needed it.

'How is Ben Mathers?' he asked.

'He came for dinner just before John and Sue were married, but he's gone to talk over a new book with a fellow historian. What a shame. I think you will miss seeing each other.'

The motorway unfolded under slim single-span bridges and past lovely farm-land. 'This is beautiful country,' he said. 'I love the freshness after our arid rocks, and the beauty of the children.' They were passing a school playground, now empty, but two children swung on a gate.

'The Greek children are adorable,' said Samantha.

'You think so?' He looked pleased. 'I thought that a career woman as cool and detached as you would have no time to notice such domestic details.'

'I can have a career and still love children,' she said.

He leaned back, an enigmatic smile touching his mouth. 'If you married, you would have no need of a career. What happens when you marry, Samantha? You will have to give up all this façade of professionalism and concentrate on your husband, your home and children, just as women have done and will do until the end of time.'

'It might be so in your country, but it doesn't follow here. A woman can have both and make a success of them without having to choose. That's where our lives are different.' She spoke sadly, knowing the gulf between them and almost seeing Cassiami's face in the driving mirror. 'Cassiami will give up everything for marriage, but I shall have a career and marry when the time is right, if I am in love.'

'Cassiami gives up nothing,' he said sharply.

Samantha stopped the car by the drive to the old barn. The conversation was on dangerous subjects and she took him to see the old car. If anything, it looked even worse now that parts of it were covered with grease, but Rhexenor caught his breath.

'It is rather a wreck, isn't it? I can't think why the Japanese who came here was so keen. John told me to show it to anyone interested, but really! It must be beyond renovation.'

'You saw my Bugatti? That was as bad as this before John and his team made it come back to life. Ah, no, you wouldn't remember.' He looked up at the blackened rafters. 'It was in here, in that corner.' His eyes held a tender memory and her heart felt like breaking. He recalled the barn and the old car, but he couldn't remember the girl who was almost a woman, weeping in the old car. He smoothed the door and his hand came away, greasy.

'Wipe your hand on this,' she said. 'And keep away until you put some overalls over that suit.' He looked incongruous in a smartly cut lightweight suit and poplin shirt of pale grey against the grimy walls of the barn. 'Neither of us is dressed for this,' she said, laughing. He gave back the soiled rag and she picked it up by one edge, trying to seem as if she wanted to avoid touching the grease, but knowing that any contact with the man who was even more than her dreams would be dangerous. 'I'll make that coffee before you go on to the pub. I believe that Sue booked you in at the Swan?'

'Yes.' He followed her into the house and smiled when he saw the fresh flowers everywhere, the bright silver and the red Virginia creeper leaves arranged in shallow bowls. 'This is a home,' he said.

'An English home,' she corrected. 'You have the most magnificent home I've seen, but quite different.'

'The atmosphere could be the same,' he said, 'It needs an injection of happiness, of love...'

'It had a good atmosphere,' said

Samantha. 'The room with the courtyard seemed...' She opened the door to the kitchen. 'Go through and see the garden while I put coffee in the filter.' He hesitated in the doorway. 'Are you hungry? I can get you something to eat here or you can have dinner at the Swan. They do very good meals there.' Something in his eyes made her turn away.

'Have dinner with me later, Samantha.' The voice held a caress and her spine tingled.

'Coffee now before I drive you to the Swan, and I'd like to have dinner with you, Rhex.' She hoped that she spoke with the right mixture of formality and friendliness, a courier being nice to a valued client. 'Sit in that chair. That's John's favourite one. You must be tired after hot flights, and I suppose Athens is at boiling point. The temperature was high yesterday in the weather chart.'

He sat down obediently, folding his hands over his chest. 'Is this better? Do you prefer me as an invalid, Samantha? Does it make me safer?' The glint of wickedness was back and she fled to make the coffee. She pushed cakes on to a plate and nearly broke one of the best cups. She took a deep breath and went back into the sitting room. He was standing by a photograph of her, taken when she was about thirteen, dressed in navy blue shorts and with her hair tied back in a pigtail, with a pony and a dog. The picture had been there for so long that she hadn't really looked at it for years, but he was gazing at it with a soft smile on his lips.

'That was a terrible snap. John wouldn't let me tear it up,' she said.

'It's beautiful,' he said. 'And you look quite good, too!'

'That pony was a rogue. He had a nasty habit of sneaking up and biting.'

As they drank coffee, the tension between them grew. Verbal fencing made them smile in a guarded manner and Samantha wished that she hadn't suggested coffee in the house alone together. She took the coffee cups back to the kitchen and went to fetch a short jacket of silk to match the suit. He looked at her almost sternly, as if he disapproved, but she knew that she looked very good.

'I'll leave my bags in my room if you'd wait in the bar for me,' he said. 'Perhaps you could tell the restaurant staff that we shall need a table for two.'

She went into the bar that she had so often used for meeting friends, where the cronies of John's racing days met when he invited them for weekends and where she had gone with Max in the days before he had shown his real character and lost her trust for ever. She stiffened. Max was there at the bar, lazily regarding her.

'Well, well, look who's here,' he said. 'Little Samantha, still in her wedding-day clothes. Can't you forgive Sue for taking your daddie away, dear?' The insolent sneer could be heard across the room and she knew with a sinking heart that he was drunk.

'That's enough, Max,' she said firmly.

'Waiting for someone? Or has your historian stood you up?'

'I'm waiting for a friend of John's who wants to buy the vintage car in the barn,' she said, as calmly as she could.

'And what about your tame historian? Named the day, have you? John said there was nothing in it, but I ought to know how the guy feels.' He came closer. 'Or are you playing hard to get with him, too?'

'John was right. Ben is just a friend I met on holiday. He's one of the nicest men I've met, but we are friends, Max, nothing more.'

'So you're in that big old house all alone, are you? Perhaps I should drop by later and cheer you up?'

'If you were sober, you wouldn't dare talk to me like that,' said Samantha angrily. He had been edging towards her all the time they were talking, and the rest of the bar crowd could no longer hear their words.

'Having trouble?' said a steely voice

behind her. Rhexenor stood a head higher than Max, his shoulders set in passive strength, his eyes blazing. Max looked up, scared.

'It's all right – he's drunk,' said Samantha.

Rhexenor put a gentle hand on the man's shoulder and patted it. 'Listen, my friend, you will leave this lady alone. She is my concern and you will answer to me if she is annoyed in any way.' He turned away, put a possessive hand under her elbow and took her into the dining room.

'Thank you, Rhex, but I can handle him.' She saw the real anger in his eyes. 'He tried once... But I think he's learned a lesson. It's just talk, now.'

'I will have no talk.' He held the chair for her and she had the illusion of being enfolded in a protective cloak of gentle strength.

'Don't be angry with him. He's not worth it, Rhex.'

The waiter brought the menu. 'I'm hungry,' she said. 'What are you eating?'

Rhexenor gazed at her with a mixture of irritation and amusement. 'All right, we'll eat and then we'll talk. I'm not angry with him; I'm angry with you!'

Throughout the meal they said little, but a band of awareness was almost tangible across the table. He's carrying his responsibilities towards the daughter of his host too far, she thought. He's really piling on the protector of women role since he got himself engaged to Cassiami. She smiled bleakly. He's salving his conscience by being ultra correct towards me to wipe out what he said on the catamaran – 'I want you. I want you.' She ate fruit salad and wondered what he wanted to say to her that made his mouth so stern. He has to tell me about Cassiami and knows that I think he is a philanderer with other women and that he would seduce me, given a chance and a time, she realised.

They went into the lounge for coffee and liqueurs, and Max had gone.

'We shall leave the car here and I will walk

back to the house with you,' he said firmly.

'He's gone home. His car isn't in the car park.'

'He may have it parked by the garage,' Rhex said patiently. The night air held a promise of autumn and lacked the exhilaration of early frosts, giving a sadness to the waving treetops. Rhex drew her hand through the crook of his arm and they walked close together. She wanted to draw away. It was agony to be treated as a casual friend. It was easier when he disliked her. The moon hung low and the misty edges of the fields were silvered.

'Is it a hunter's moon?' asked Samantha, to break the silence.

'In Greece we have only the Goddess Phoebe, who sails over the night. She is our huntress and enchantress, ensnaring us and making us mad with her cool beauty, as you do.' He stopped by a shadowy bush and cupped her chin in his hand and kissed her lightly.

'You mustn't,' she breathed.

'Why did you stay away from me, Samantha. I called for you and dreamed that you were by my bed.'

'I – I did come and Cassiami sent me away.' He stiffened. 'You were unconscious and I wasn't allowed to see you again before I came home.'

'No message? Nothing?'

'I sent you some flowers and a card,' she said.

'And they never came.' He murmured something in Greek.

'What did you say? I couldn't stay... They said I had no right and you were to marry Cassiami.'

'Did I say so?' His anger was terrible. 'Did *she* tell you that? Just as she told me that you were engaged to the man who looks at museums! At least I have your drunken friend to thank for telling me that you are not engaged. Why did you tell me you were?'

'I didn't. I said that when someone – meaning you – was engaged...' She couldn't finish her words as his mouth found hers

283

and she was swept into his arms.

'Little fool, darling little fool. You do love me,' he said in triumph, as she drew away shyly and looked up to see if he was still angry. His eyes glowed with the discovery of the treasure of her love. His arms rejoiced in the yielding of her slim body to his care, with love and ecstasy and complete trust.

'Rhex, if you don't love her, why did you go to Athens with her?'

'To get rid of her for good! She tried to organise my life and I sent her back to her brother. I have never wanted her or loved her. I have never wanted or loved any woman as I love you.' He laughed. 'And your father is away. I cannot ask his permission to marry his daughter.'

'Ever heard of women's rights?' she said, with a hint of mischief.

'This time, I bow to that. Will you give your consent? Will you give yourself to me, Samantha?'

'When John and Sue return. Yes, I'll marry you, Rhex.'

'And it wasn't a dream that Nausicaa came and told me she loved me?'

Her face was suffused with blushes. 'You knew it was me. You heard.'

He kissed her again, with tenderness and the solemnity of commitment. 'Let's say the turtles spoke of it, in a little whisper.'

The publishers hope that this book has given you enjoyable reading. Large Print Books are especially designed to be as easy to see and hold as possible. If you wish a complete list of our books please ask at your local library or write directly to:

Magna Large Print Books
Magna House, Long Preston,
Skipton, North Yorkshire.
BD23 4ND

This Large Print Book for the partially sighted, who cannot read normal print, is published under the auspices of
THE ULVERSCROFT FOUNDATION